THE CALM AFTER THE STORM

I woke up after midnight. The storm had passed.

It was silent. Dead silent.

It must have been the total silence after the wind and the rain that awakened me.

And it seemed cold in my room—an indescribable, bone-numbing cold, as if the warmth was being sucked out of my body.

The sky was cloudless now and the moon was full and shone eerily through the window beside my bed.

The sobbing, when it came, was distant and faint. I sat up in bed and listened. Was it Peter, having a nightmare?

No, that wasn't Peter.

It was a woman. A woman weeping as if her heart was breaking.

Don't miss these terrifying thrillers by
Edgar Award–Nominee
Bebe Faas Rice

Class Trip
Class Trip II
Love You to Death
The Listeners
Music From the Dead

Available from HarperPaperbacks

MUSIC FROM THE DEAD

Bebe Faas Rice

HarperPaperbacks
A Division of HarperCollinsPublishers

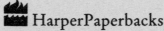

HarperPaperbacks

A Division of HarperCollins*Publishers*
10 East 53rd Street, New York, N.Y. 10022-5299

This is a work of fiction. The characters, incidents, and
dialogues are products of the author's imagination and are not to
be construed as real. Any resemblance to actual events or
persons, living or dead, is entirely coincidental.

ISBN 0-06-106457-2

HarperCollins®, 📖®, and HarperPaperbacks™
are trademarks of HarperCollins*Publishers,* Inc.

Cover illustration by Jeff Walker

First printing: April 1997

Printed in the United States of America

Visit HarperPaperbacks on the World Wide Web at
http://www.harpercollins.com/paperbacks

❖ 10 9 8 7 6 5 4 3 2 1

To my family

MUSIC FROM THE DEAD

PROLOGUE

I found a photo of Stoneycraig yesterday, the only one I have of that tormented, haunt-ridden house overlooking the sea.

I'd taken it myself, that first day, when we pulled up in the driveway. At the time, I'd thought that Stoneycraig was beautiful—so old and mellow-looking—and I wanted to get a quick shot of it to send to friends back home.

It was a cold, gray morning. The sea was dark, with angry, tossing whitecaps. A sharp breeze blew toward us from the water, and I could hear the screaming of gulls as they flocked inland before the wind.

Picking up my camera, I left the van and ran out on the long lawn that sloped downward to the edge of the cliff. Then I turned, pointing the lens at the front of the house. I wanted to get it all—the fat stone chimneys on either end, the round, columned porch, and the ancient purple wisteria that grew wild and unchecked up one side of the house.

The morning sun was half-hidden by tattered, patchy clouds. I waited until the gusting wind blew them away, and then I snapped the shutter.

When the picture developed, I told myself that the dark, human-looking shape in the upper window was just a trick of the uncertain light. A reflection on the glass. That no one had been up there, looking down on us. After all, hadn't the house been empty when we entered it later?

But I know now who'd been watching us that morning from the great, arched window of the landing.

It was She.

Had our coming brought her back from the grave, or had She always been there, waiting . . . watching?

1

"Here we are, Marnie," Peter said, hunching over the steering wheel and peering left and right. "Pedlar's Green."

Pedlar's Green. The village looked as old-fashioned as its name. A cluster of white houses fronted the traditional New England village green. Ahead, a narrow street lined with shops and stores and huge, overhanging trees sloped down to the water.

Mr. Maltravers, the local real-estate agent, had given the place quite a write-up in his letter to Dad.

"Pedlar's Green," he'd written, "is a charming little picture-postcard village. Seaside Maine at its very best."

Well, we'd see about that.

We hit a bump in the road, and the red minivan bounced. A couple of boxes stacked in the rear fell over. Peter's lacrosse stick slipped forward and whacked me in the head. I turned around and shoved it back into place.

A few months ago I would have yelled at Peter to slow down, that the police in these picture-postcard villages were always ready to nail out-of-towners.

In return, he would have told me to shut up and mind my own business, and what made me such a big expert on driving, anyway, when I'd flunked driver's ed twice?

But that was then. Before he went away. Now we were being polite to each other for the first time in our lives.

Peter Van Zandt, my cousin and formerly my very best friend and confidant, seemed, well, *different* somehow these days. Or was it just me?

Actually, Peter isn't really my cousin. His grandfather married my grandmother's sister-in-law, or something like that. It's very complicated. Although we aren't blood kin, our families have always acted like we were, and Peter and I grew up in each other's houses, being treated like family. I can't remember a time when Peter wasn't an important part of my life.

My father is Lewis B. McKay, a political writer and newspaper columnist. We live in a large old townhouse in Washington, D.C. Peter's father is Professor Quenton Van Zandt, the famous archaeologist attached to the Smithsonian Institution. They live down the street from us, in a house just like ours. Our mothers went to school together. Like I said, this thing between Peter and me goes way back.

My mother died when I was a baby, so Peter's mother, Aunt Florrie, has always been sort of a mother substitute to me. I don't have any pictures in my baby book that don't include Peter, hamming it up and hogging the playpen.

We're only a few months apart in age, too, but Peter, who turned seventeen last spring, would be going into his senior year in the fall, while I, at sixteen, would be a junior. His being in a higher grade has always given him the idea that he's smarter and more mature than I am. Wrong! Peter acts like a total fool sometimes, especially around girls. I wish I had a nickel for every time I've had to give him womanly advice about love or rescue him from the clutches of some designing female.

Girls have always had this thing for Peter. Even my best friends keep telling me what a hunkerino he is with those blue eyes and sandy hair and wide shoulders. Funny I'd never noticed it before.

Until now, that is.

Yes, squinting sideways at him as he piloted his clapped-out red minivan through the streets of Pedlar's Green, I was beginning to see what they meant.

His profile seemed sharper, craggier, than it used to be. His chin had gotten bonier or something. And I liked his new nose. He'd broken it playing soccer a couple of months ago, and it had healed with just the teensiest little hump which was kind of sexy-looking, actually, even though Aunt Florrie kept trying to talk him into cosmetic surgery.

It must have been the long separation that made me look at him with new eyes.

Last December, Uncle Quent and Aunt Florrie went off on an archaeological dig and took Peter along. Peter usually stays with Dad and me when his parents travel during the school year, but this time they were going to England, to excavate a cluster of Roman ruins that had been uncovered up by the Scottish border.

"Five months in a fine old British prep school will be a wonderful Enriching Experience for Peter," Aunt Florrie declared. Enriching Experiences have always been a real biggie with her.

"But I don't want to be enriched," Peter had argued desperately. At the time, he had a massive crush on Debbi Sue Tipton, local love goddess, and was afraid she'd find someone new while he was away.

He was right. Debbi Sue, whose two-digit IQ matched her bust measurement, and who dotted the *i* in her name with a little heart, did find someone else while he was away. Todd "Swifty" Sweeny. The "Swifty" nickname had nothing to do with athletic ability. Well, not the sort of athletic ability you'd associate with organized sports, anyway.

In spite of his protests, Peter wound up spending five ghastly months at Ecclecleuch Manor, a three hundred-year-old boarding school over the Scottish border in a remote, hilly area where, in ancient times, the clans used to meet every now and then to wipe each other out.

All Peter learned at Ecclecleuch, he said, was what to wear under a kilt, what to do if you met the queen, and how not to get your teeth knocked out in a game of British rugby.

He never *did* tell me what he'd worn under his uniform kilt.

All he'd say in this shrill, hysterical voice was, "Marnie, it was like five months in a Siberian prison! I had to break the ice in my bedside basin to wash in the morning. Pitchers and basins, can you believe it? I felt like Oliver Twist. Bells ringing at the crack of dawn. Oatmeal for breakfast. And those crazy teachers talking Latin! They actually expected me to know what they were saying. I thought Latin was a dead language!"

Peter usually wobbled out of control at this point.

Anyway, here we were, the two of us, in Pedlar's Green, Maine.

How, you may ask, did this happen?

Well, I'll tell you.

My father had a mild heart attack a couple of months ago. It was just a little one, but it scared us all half to death.

It was a warning, our family doctor said. A sign that Dad had to slow down. Avoid stress. Get away from the pressure cooker of Washington politics. Take a long vacation.

Dad had been collecting notes for a book on Vietnam for several years. He decided this was the perfect time to do something with them, to go off for the summer to a quiet, secluded spot and write his book.

Through a Washington Realtor's contacts, he'd rented, sight unseen, an old house on the rocky seacoast of Maine.

The house even had a name. Stoneycraig. It sat

on a high cliff overlooking the sea, not far from Pedlar's Green. And it had a pre–Civil War history. Supposedly it had been a stop on the Underground Railroad, the route organized to help runaway slaves escape into Canada. From Stoneycraig the fugitives had been taken across the water to the Canadian province of New Brunswick and freedom.

I can't say I liked the idea of spending an entire summer in some creepy, rundown old house, but Dad's the only parent I've got, and I didn't want to lose him. So, if the doctor prescribed a summer in Pedlar's Green, I'd just have to grin and go along with it.

Besides, Norman, my on-again, off-again boyfriend, wouldn't be around Washington this summer, anyway. He'd been hired as a counselor at a summer camp in West Virginia. I didn't much like being left behind while he spent the summer at Camp Weechiwatchi surrounded (probably!) by gorgeous girls in bikinis. At least this way I'd be going somewhere, too, even if Pedlar's Green turned out to be the armpit of the universe.

"You're better off away from that creep, Marnie," Peter had said. "I don't know what you see in him."

Peter has never had anything good to say about Norman, but he was worse now that he was home from merrie olde Scotland.

That's another thing. He seemed to be looking at me a little differently these days, too. I'd actually caught him staring thoughtfully at my legs a couple of times. This was definitely a change in our buddy-buddy relationship. Maybe being locked up for five months in a remote, all-male boarding school does this to guys. In a way it was flattering, yet it was kind of unnerving at the same time.

Anyway, since Dad couldn't leave Washington for another week, it was decided that Peter would drive me up to Pedlar's Green, help me get settled in and stick around until Dad got there. Then he'd take off for Canada. His folks had friends in Montreal, and Peter hoped to get in some lacrosse with a summer league up there. Lacrosse is his big love. Next to girls, that is. His parents were letting him go as a reward for surviving his Enriching Experience at Ecclecleuch Manor.

Peter slowed the van to a crawl as we drove past the thin-spired white church that bordered the green. "Don't tell me there's no supermarket in this town," he said, glancing around anxiously. "I've got to pick up something for supper tonight."

"What do you mean?" I asked. "Dad said he made arrangements for a live-in housekeeper at Stoneycraig. Won't she be doing all the cooking?"

"Not when she sees how good I am," Peter said.

"*Good?*" I echoed. "The only thing I've ever seen you cook is s'mores. And you always burn the marshmallows."

"My consciousness has recently been raised," Peter replied with a modest smile. "You are now looking at a gourmet cook, Marnie."

"Since when?"

"Since Ecclecleuch," he replied. His left eye twitched. It always did that when he mentioned his British alma mater.

"You mean they even made you *cook* in that place?"

"No, but the food was so terrible I bought a gourmet cookbook at a local bookshop and read it every night to cheer myself up." He eyed me sideways over that new, sexy little hump on his nose. "And that's where I discovered an incredible culinary secret."

"A *what* kind of secret?"

"Culinary. Pertaining to the kitchen. It comes from an old Latin word. What's the matter with you, Marnie? Don't you know anything?"

Aha. Maybe the old Peter Van Zandt had not totally disappeared, after all.

"Okay. So what's the big culinary secret?" I asked.

Peter lowered his voice confidentially. "That gourmet cooking is basically cooking with sauces."

"No kidding, Dick Tracy," I retorted with a sneer, forgetting my new boy-girl politeness. "You had to go all the way to Scotland to figure *that* one out?"

Peter ignored my sarcasm. "I've been doing a lot of cooking since I got home," he said earnestly. "I've watched those chefs on TV do their fancy stuff, and I've come up with some pretty basic shortcuts. I don't make all those tricky, complicated sauces. I use cream soups instead. Plain, old-fashioned soup right out of a can."

"Listen, Peter," I said nervously. "Maybe we ought to just let that housekeeper—"

"Hey, here's a grocery store," Peter exclaimed. He yanked sharply at the steering wheel and pulled nose in before a small shop with a sign reading ABBOTT'S GROCERIES in the window. "It's not a supermarket, but it's bound to have canned soup."

His voice turned soft and dreamy. "I thought I'd do gumboburgers on toasted sesame rolls tonight. I might even throw in a few chunks of Mexican Velveeta for that little *soupçon* of unexpected flavor."

A *soupçon* of Mexican Velveeta? This cooking thing seemed to come with a whole new vocabulary.

The grocery store was empty when we entered, but a plump-faced, older looking man bustled out of the back room, wiping his hands. He introduced himself as Mr. Abbott. I'd never had a grocery store owner introduce himself by name before, and I liked that personal touch.

Mr. Abbott insisted on fetching all the items on our list himself. He even wiped the dust off the can of chicken gumbo soup before placing it in the grocery bag. "We don't have much call for this one," he explained, smiling apologetically. "Folks around here are pretty old-fashioned. They usually stick to chicken noodle."

Behind his gold-rimmed spectacles, his eyes were light brown and friendly. "You kids passing through?" he asked. "Where are you headed?"

"My father's rented a summer place up here," I told him.

Mr. Abbott cocked his head like a curious dog. "In town? We don't have many summer people this year. I thought I met all of them." He laughed. "I'm the only grocery store in town. Everybody comes in here sooner or later."

He wrapped the hamburger we'd ordered in waxed paper and set it inside a smaller bag. "So where will you two be staying?"

"We're not *in* Pedlar's Green, actually," Peter explained. "We're a couple miles out of town, at this place called Stoneycraig."

"Oh . . . Stoneycraig," Mr. Abbott said slowly with a slight frown. He was silent for a moment. Then he said, "I heard someone was renting the house for the summer, but I thought it was a writer fella who wanted to be alone. Some big-city guy."

"That's my father," I said, trying not to laugh at his description of Dad. "He's coming up in a week or so. The whole thing happened kind of fast. We were lucky to get a house on such short notice."

"It's always easy to rent Stoneycraig," Mr. Abbott said, and hastily added, "I mean, it's a big house and we don't have a call for that sort of thing around here."

"We haven't seen the house yet," I told him. "Our Realtor back in Washington wrote to someone he knows up here. That's how we got it."

"Mr. Maltravers is the only Realtor in Pedlar's Green," Mr. Abbott said.

"That's the name," Peter exclaimed.

"Maltravers. Where can we find him? We need to pick up the key."

Mr. Abbott wedged a bunch of green onions lengthwise into one of the grocery bags and folded the top over carefully. "His office is right down the street, next to the Maltravers First Bank of Maine. You can't miss it."

"You mean he owns the bank, too?" Peter asked.

Mr. Abbott shook his head. "No, but his father does. The bank's been in the family for several generations. The Maltraverses have lived in this area since the seventeen hundreds."

As Peter and I gathered up our groceries, Mr. Abbott leaned over the counter and cleared his throat. "Listen," he said. "You two look like real nice, sensible kids. So let me give you a little friendly advice. Don't go paying attention to any crazy stories you might hear about Stoneycraig, okay?"

Peter and I exchanged puzzled glances. "What crazy stories?" I asked.

Mr. Abbott made a helpless little gesture with his hands.

"What stories?" I repeated.

"Old houses always have a lot of stories connected with them, don't they?" Mr. Abbott replied evasively. "And in a town like Pedlar's Green, people like to . . . kind of . . . add to them. I'm just telling you not to pay any mind to anything you might hear about Stoneycraig, if you know what I mean."

No, I didn't know what he meant.

I started to say so, but just then an elderly

woman hobbled into the store and Mr. Abbott turned to help her.

I cast a quick glance over my shoulder at Mr. Abbott as we left. He was saying something to the woman in a low voice.

I had a funny feeling he was talking about us.

2

"What was that all about?" Peter asked, jamming the groceries into the rear of the van.

I shrugged. "Who knows? Mr. Abbott said the house is old. A lot's happened there. Family stuff, I suppose. We'll have to ask the housekeeper. She ought to know."

Peter rolled his eyes at me. "Maybe Pedlar's Green is one of those towns where everybody's related to everybody else, and they keep loony old aunts locked up in attics."

"Thanks a lot," I snapped. "That really makes me feel better about spending the entire summer in this dump while you're off in Canada having fun."

I peered up and down the deserted street. "This place looks like something out of *The Twilight Zone*, Peter. Do you realize we haven't seen a movie theater? Or a pizza parlor? Or even a video rental store?"

"No, I guess we haven't," Peter admitted. "But

don't make your mind up about Pedlar's Green town until you've talked to Mr. Maltravers. There might be a lot of fun stuff going on around here that you don't know about. I mean, maybe it turns into a tourist spot like Nantucket or something."

"I doubt it," I said dismally, watching a big black dog wander out into the middle of the road and lie down. "I'm starting to get a funny feeling that not a lot of cars come through here."

Peter shoved the last bag of groceries into the van, slammed the door, and eyed me sternly. "Listen, Marnie, I hope you aren't going to talk like that in front of your dad. Uncle Lewis needs you right now. That heart attack thing scared him more than he wants to admit. I overheard Mom and Dad the other night. They said Uncle Lewis feels he hasn't been spending enough time with you these past months, what with his schedule and all, and he wants this summer to be special. Just the two of you, working on the book together."

"But Peter—"

"Put yourself in his shoes," Peter urged. "He's going to be okay, but his heart attack has made him think about priorities, and he's got this idea he's been neglecting you for his work."

"That's not true!"

Peter shrugged. "I know that, and you know that, but Uncle Lewis doesn't. He told Dad he wants to give you some real quality time this summer."

"Oh boy," I groaned. "I know what his idea of quality time is—him dictating and me typing away madly at a computer."

"So what's the alternative, Marnie? You sulking around, making him miserable and nagging him into another heart attack?"

"Of course not," I snapped. "You know I'm no whiner."

"Then shut up and put your money where your mouth is," he said, sounding like the old pre-Ecclecleuch Peter, the Peter who'd been giving me lectures over the years on everything from how to whistle to how not to act on a date.

It was kind of nice having the old bossy Peter back.

"Why are you grinning at me like that?" he asked suspiciously.

I cocked my head. "I think you're right about not having your nose fixed. That's a real macho-looking bump."

"Good grief, Marnie," he complained. "Don't you ever listen to anything I say?"

Maltravers Realty was a short walk from Abbott's Grocery. We set off down Merchant Street in the direction Mr. Abbott had indicated.

We were in the older section of the village now. The paved sidewalk gave way to cobblestones. Narrow houses and shops pressed up close against each other. Ahead was the cove with its creaking, weather-beaten piers and squawking seagulls. A cluster of tethered sailboats bobbed and danced on the gray, choppy water.

Maltravers First Bank of Maine sat on the corner of Merchant and Water streets, down by the cove. It was a tall, flat-fronted stone building with high windows and the date 1879 engraved in a square of marble over the door. Next to it, in a small blue house with white shutters, was Maltravers Realty.

The secretary at the desk in the front office looked up and smiled when we entered.

"You must be the Stoneycraig renters," she said, pushing back her chair. "Mr. Maltravers has been expecting you."

When she came from behind her desk to lead us into Mr. Maltravers's office, I saw that she was wearing baggy polyester slacks and running shoes. Back home, real-estate saleswomen wear power suits and pumps. When she wasn't looking, I raised my eyebrows meaningfully at Peter. He frowned and shook his head. Peter says I'm a snob about clothes.

Mr. Maltravers's office was a real I-love-me affair. The walls were covered with plaques and framed pictures of him shaking hands with important-looking people and receiving trophies and awards. I didn't see any sign of a Mrs. Maltravers in the pictures.

On a far wall were massed photos of him at a younger age, wearing a football uniform. In some he was leaping up, making what looked like spectacular midair catches. In others he was clutching a football and running, head down, one arm thrust out to fend off tacklers. A couple of big colored pictures showed him surrounded by pretty girls in cheerleader outfits. They were all gazing up at him adoringly. No wonder. He was pretty studly in those days.

Those days were long gone now. Mr. Maltravers was at least as old as my father, except that Dad always worked out and watched his diet and Mr. Maltravers obviously didn't. He looked like he'd put on a lot of weight since he scored his last touchdown.

He was still rather good-looking, though, and still a man with the ladies, judging by the way his secretary batted her eyes at him, but his blond hair was thinning and streaked with gray, and he combed it up from the back and over his bald spot in an elaborate sweep.

"You're the kids who will be living in the old Hadley place, right?" he asked, putting his coffee mug on his desk and giving us a big, friendly grin. He gestured to a couple of ladder-back chairs. "Sit down. Take the weight off. I figured you two would probably spend the night down the road apiece and come in this morning. Coffee? Soda?"

We both shook our heads.

"Hadley place?" I asked, perching on the edge of one of the chairs and slipping off my shoulder bag. "Dad said the house he rented is called Stoneycraig."

Mr. Maltravers leaned back in his swivel chair and put his hands behind his head. "Same thing," he said cheerfully. "Stoneycraig belongs to a local man named Matt Hadley. An ancestor of his built it in the early eighteen hundreds. It's been in his family ever since."

"We got the impression that the owner hasn't lived in the house for a long time," Peter said.

"He hasn't," Mr. Maltravers told us. "He rents it out now and then, mainly to summer folks like yourselves. Matt lives in town now, in that big house on the green. You probably saw it when you drove past."

"You mean the one with the columns?" I asked.

"Yeah, the fancy one. It's the biggest house in town. The Hadleys have always had a lot of money. They've lived in Pedlar's Green almost as long as the Maltraverses."

He looked over at Peter and winked. "Matt's got a pretty little granddaughter. Her name is Clare, and she's just about your age. I could introduce you if you're interested."

Peter blushed and shuffled his feet. "I'm only going to be around for a couple of days, then I'm headed for Canada, but Marnie's been hoping there'd be some kids her age up here."

Mr. Maltravers shook his head. "I'm afraid not. Most of the young people get summer jobs at the resorts down the coast. There's not much up here for them, come summer."

He looked from me to Peter and then back again at me. "Your dad said you two were cousins, but you don't look anything alike."

Peter and I exchanged a quick glance. Dad always told people Peter was related to us. He said it saved a lot of explaining. It would in a small, gossipy town like Pedlar's Green, anyway.

"We, uh, take after different sides of the family," I said, looking down.

"Yeah," Peter chimed in with a big, innocent smile. "Marnie looks just like Grandma. And she's got the temper that goes with all that red hair, too."

I glared at Peter. He knows I hate my hair. Not only is it red, but it's thick and curly and you can't do much with it except wear it like a burning bush.

In an attempt to change the subject I asked, "Why doesn't Mr. Hadley live at Stoneycraig, Mr. Maltravers, if it's a family home?"

Mr. Maltravers sat upright. His swivel chair squeaked. He put his elbows on the desk and clasped his hands together. "That's a long story," he said slowly, frowning.

Peter and I looked at each other in alarm. First Mr. Abbott and his weird hints about Stoneycraig, and now Mr. Maltravers. What was going on here, anyway?

"Is . . . is something wrong with the house?" Peter asked hesitantly. "According to what you told Uncle Lewis in your letter, it's clean and comfortable and—"

Mr. Maltravers interrupted him. "Oh, it's a nice house, all right. It's just that Stoneycraig has kind of a sad history."

For some reason, a cold prickle ran down my spine.

"What do you mean?" I asked suspiciously.

"Nothing that could possibly affect you, of course," Mr. Maltravers said hurriedly, avoiding my gaze. "It's just that the house holds some unhappy memories for Matt Hadley."

Peter narrowed his eyes. He looked older, more mature at that moment. I was glad he was with me.

"Maybe you ought to tell us about the house now, Mr. Maltravers," he said, "before we—my cousin—moves in. Mr. Abbott at the grocery store said something about us hearing what he called 'crazy stories' connected with Stoneycraig. It might be better if we heard them from you, if you don't mind."

Mr. Maltravers appeared to think that one over. Finally he said, "Okay. Why not? Mr. Abbott was right. People like to talk about the past in this town, so you're bound to find out sooner or later, anyway."

"Find out *what*?" I asked.

"About Matt Hadley's daughter," Mr. Maltravers explained.

He settled back in his chair again. "Matt only had one child. Ellen. He thought the sun rose and set on that girl."

Mr. Maltravers paused and looked at his desk, his eyes veiled. "A lot of us did. She was really something. Beautiful. Sweet. She had everything going for her."

"So what happened to her?" I prompted.

"What happened to her?" Mr. Maltravers echoed, his voice rising shrilly. "She went off to some artsy college in New York City and came back married to a no-good bum—a songwriter named Stephen D'Amato. She could have had anybody. Instead, she settled for that D'Amato jerk. Well, at least he married her before the baby came."

"*That's* the terrible secret?" I demanded incredulously. "That Mr. Hadley's daughter married a songwriter and had a baby that may or may not have been started before the wedding? Big deal! Is this town on an alien planet or something?"

Mr. Maltravers shook his head. "No, wait.

There's more. Matt didn't much care for D'Amato, but he tried to make the best of a bad deal. He gave Stoneycraig to Ellen as a wedding present and moved into town. Said he wanted to pass the house on to the next generation."

He lowered his voice. "But when Ellen was in the hospital having the baby, D'Amato ran off and left her." He shook his head in disbelief. "Can you imagine a man deserting his wife at a time like that? And a wife like Ellen, too."

"No," I admitted. "But I guess it happens, even in a place like Pedlar's Green."

"Anyway," Mr. Maltravers said, pushing back his chair and standing up, "that was more than sixteen years ago, and D'Amato has never come back. Soon after he left, Ellen . . . died. The whole business nearly broke her father's heart. He adopted Ellen's baby, Clare, so she'd legally be a Hadley, not a D'Amato like her father. He can't stand the sound of the name. Even now. That's how much he hated the man."

"And Mr. Hadley never moved back into Stoneycraig?" Peter asked.

"No. He said it reminded him too much of Ellen and what happened to her. So he's kept Stoneycraig rented all these years, whenever he can, usually to summer people."

He opened a desk drawer and started pawing around in it. "I've got the key here somewhere. Ah, here it is." He pulled it out and handed it to me. "No need for me to go with you. Mrs. Gleason, the housekeeper, ought to be there when you arrive. And Stoneycraig is easy to find. You can't miss it. Ask my secretary for directions when you leave."

"Before we do, though, Mr. Maltravers," I began, "there's one thing I still don't understand."

He closed his desk drawer and looked at me expectantly, eyebrows raised.

"Those stories that people are supposed to be telling about Stoneycraig," I said. "The ones Mr. Abbott called 'crazy.' Why are people still talking about what happened after all these years?"

"They *are* crazy stories," he said with a shrug. "Not much happens around here, and people like to gossip, so . . ." He shrugged again.

"Uh, Mr. Maltravers," Peter began. "About Ellen Hadley dying. I'm kind of—you know—curious. Did she . . . did Ellen die in that house?"

"Oh no," I gasped. "I hadn't thought of *that*. Don't tell me we have to live in a house where somebody *died!*"

Mr. Maltravers shook his head. "No, not at all. Like I told you, you have nothing to worry about. I give you my word. Ellen Hadley definitely did not die in that house."

I would remember later that Mr. Maltravers had put a peculiar emphasis on the word *in*.

A single-lane road led out of the village and wound its way up to a windy plateau high above Pedlar's Green. And there, on a rocky point of land with the sea on three sides, sat Stoneycraig.

Stoneycraig! I'll always remember how I felt the first time I saw it.

Something about the house reminded me of *Wuthering Heights,* a book I'd read last year for English lit. Maybe it was Stoneycraig's age and size, and the way it sat there alone and windswept, surrounded by those wild, overgrown gardens that made it look like a house from another time. A house with a secret.

I fell in love with it on the spot.

"Wow," I managed to gasp. "I had no idea it was going to look like *this!*"

Peter parked the van and we got out, our feet making scrunching sounds on the crushed white seashells that paved the driveway.

I could tell by the expression on his face that Peter was every bit as impressed by Stoneycraig as I was. "This is just what the doctor ordered for Uncle Lewis," he finally said, nodding his head in approval. "It's the perfect place for him to hole up and write his book."

He took a deep breath. "You can even smell the sea from up here!"

I sniffed. A fresh sea breeze blew toward us, mixed with the pleasant scent of grass and wildflowers. "All that fresh air will probably make us sleep like logs tonight," I said.

I was dead wrong on that one, as we found out soon afterward.

Stoneycraig faced the sea, overlooking a long lawn that sloped down to the cliff's edge. On one side was a slight wooded rise, on the other, a thin line of bushes. At the far end of the lawn, on the very edge of the cliff, stood a tree so old and bent that it looked like a hangman's gallows. It leaned over the sharp rocks below, its arms outstretched as if to catch the fog that crept in from the sea.

The house was built of weathered gray stone, and was wide and two-storied with huge double chimneys on each end and a round, pillared porch in front. The panes of glass in the long windows were nobbly and wavery with those round bull's-eye imperfections that meant the glass was blown by hand, and a long time ago, too.

It was a good thing Mr. Maltravers had given us a key to the house, because Mrs. Gleason, the housekeeper, wasn't there. We didn't see her car in the driveway, and when we entered the house, calling her name, there was no answer.

The inside of Stoneycraig was just as incredible as the outside.

We stood in the broad foyer, looking around.

"Upper class," Peter said in an awed voice. "Old-time upper class. Like one of those places George Washington slept in."

"Mr. Hadley has the real thing here, that's for sure," I agreed. "Look at that grandfather clock, Peter. It's like something out of a museum."

"I can't believe he actually rents this place out," Peter continued. "He must be nuts."

"And to summer people, too," I said, shaking my head in disbelief. "Can you imagine coming in here in a wet bathing suit, with sand on your feet?"

"Maybe he's hard up for ready cash," Peter suggested.

"No, I think he just wants to keep people in the house," I said. "He doesn't want to live in it, but maybe he doesn't want to sell it, either. After all, Stoneycraig's been in his family for generations."

I ran my hand over the finish of a bowfront table that stood along the wall. "And he's definitely not hard up. If he were, he'd sell all this good furniture and buy cheapo reproductions. This is the real stuff, Peter. You can always tell."

Even though Mrs. Gleason wasn't there, she'd obviously been in earlier. A bowl of freshly picked pansies stood on the table, and everything was polished and scented with lemon oil.

A curving staircase stretched from the foyer to the upper landing. From where I stood, looking up,

I could see an arched window that looked out over the sea. The reflections of the waves made a moving pattern on the ceiling whenever the sun broke through the clouds. It was hypnotic, like watching the ocean.

The living room was on one side of the foyer and the dining room on the other. Both were furnished with what looked like old family pieces and had fireplaces with carved marble mantels. Oriental carpets the color of ripe pomegranates dotted the floors. The original Mr. Hadley hadn't spared the expense, that was for sure.

The house was beautiful. And yet . . .

And yet there was something cold about it. When Peter and I called to each other from different rooms there was an echo—a spooky, lonesome sort of echo—that shouldn't have been there with all that furniture and those carpets.

We hurried into the kitchen.

It seemed warmer, more relaxed in there. Maybe that was because it was older and more roughly built than the rest of the house. The floor was made of wide pine planks. The floor-to-ceiling cupboard looked like someone had built it by hand a long time ago. Copper pots hung from the low, raftered ceiling.

"This must have been the original part of the house," I said, looking around. "You know—they'd build one big room and live in it while they added on to the house."

The most amazing part of the kitchen was its walk-in fireplace, the size of a large closet. It was faced in the same gray stone as the outside of the

house, and it had a hand-hewn beam for a mantel-
piece. You could even see the original ax marks in
the wood.

The fireplace wasn't used any more, though. A
modern gas stove had been set into it. The stove
looked small inside that stone cavern.

Peter walked into the fireplace and poked
around behind the stove. "Hey, Marnie," he called
back. His voice echoed hollowly. "There are a couple of those swinging arm things that held cooking
pots in here. Boy, is this fireplace big! What did
they roast in here, whole cows?"

"They had large families in those days," I
answered, raising my voice so he could hear. "And
they used to cook huge meals. Be glad someone put
in that stove, or we'd have to cook over an open
fire."

Peter's face appeared at the side of the stove.
"We? What's this *we* stuff?" he asked. "When I
cook, I cook solo."

"Please don't tell me you've turned into a temperamental chef," I begged.

"I've turned into a temperamental chef," he said.
"And by the way, the chef never does any of the
cleaning up. That means you've got scullery duty
this week."

"I suppose *scullery* is another word you learned
at Ecclecleuch Manor," I snapped.

"I learned a lot of words in that place," Peter
replied, his left eye twitching, "many of which I can-
not repeat in front of you. But the word *scullery*—"

I held up both hands. "Wait. Don't tell me. It
comes from the old Latin."

"Right!" Peter stared at me in pretended amazement. "Gee, Marnie. Maybe you're not as dumb as you look."

After we brought in the groceries, we set out to see the upper floor.

Some of the treads in the curving staircase creaked slightly as we ascended. On either side of the upper landing was a long hall with doors that opened out onto it, three on the left and three on the right.

We went through the three bedrooms on one side of the upper landing. They were all pretty much alike. Each was huge and high-ceilinged, with its own fireplace, sitting area, and four-poster bed. I figured Peter and I and the housekeeper would move into this side of the landing and leave the three rooms on the other side to Dad for his bedroom, library, and office.

The first two bedrooms on his side were just like ours. Mrs. Gleason had obviously done her thing up here, too, as once again everything was dusted and polished.

Then we came to the third room, the one on the end.

At first we couldn't get the door open. We rattled and twisted and jiggled the knob, but it seemed stuck. Finally, motioning me aside, Peter threw his shoulder against the door.

It popped open with a sound like a pistol shot . . . and a strange twanging, like the plucked strings of a harp.

"What was that?" Peter asked in a hoarse whisper.

We pushed the door open wider and peered fearfully around its edge.

We were in what once must have been a music room. An old piano sat in a shadowy corner. It had the look of a grand piano, yet it was rectangular, with huge, fat legs.

I pointed to the piano, laughing with relief. "That's what made the sound. When the door sprang open, it made the strings vibrate."

Peter grinned and shook his head, embarrassed. "It sure had me going there for a minute. Hey, look. It's one of those old-fashioned ones like your great-aunt Agnes used to have, remember?"

I walked over to the piano, perched on its narrow bench, and played several notes on the yellowed ivory keys. It produced a tinny, tinkling sound, as if it were only one step up from a harpsichord. I wondered how old it was. Aunt Agnes had probably told me about hers, but I guess I hadn't been listening.

Peter sneezed. "It's dusty in here!" he complained.

Leaning down, he printed his name in the dust of the leather-topped table that stood in the center of the room. "None of the other rooms are in bad shape like this," he said. "I wonder why?"

I turned away from the piano. "It's not just dusty, either," I said, gazing critically around the room—at the sofa, covered in baggy, faded chintz, and the guitar with two broken strings, propped forlornly in the corner. "It looks like nobody ever comes in here."

A five-armed silver candelabra, badly in need of polishing, sat on the piano. I tried to pick it up, but it was heavy, and it took both hands. Another antique, I supposed. Even the candles were yellowed with age and had thick pools of dust around their wicks.

Peter was still standing by the table. He'd found a drawer and pulled it open. "Hey, look at this," he said, holding up a tattered sheaf of papers. "This is the kind of paper you use when you write music. See, it's got the five lines where you put in the notes."

Suddenly I knew whose room this had been, and why it had been closed up and left to decay. "Peter," I said quietly. "This must be Stephen D'Amato's music room. This is where he wrote his songs."

Peter stared down at the papers in his hand. Then he shoved them back into the drawer and slammed it shut. "Those were all blank," he told me. "I guess he took all his songs with him when he ran off and left Ellen."

"Well, he never made it big in show biz," I said with bitter satisfaction. "I've never heard of him."

"Me neither," Peter said, "and it serves him right, the sleaze!" Suddenly he shivered. "Is it cold in here, or is it just me?"

"No, it's cold," I replied, rubbing my arms, surprised to see that they'd broken out in goose bumps. "Maybe that window over there is cracked or something."

I went over to it and held up my hand, but felt no draft. The window was in fine shape. It was even double paned. "That's funny," I said. "Why should this room be so cold when none of the other bedrooms are?"

And then this terrible, terrible feeling washed over me. It came on suddenly, too, with no warning. I guess you'd call it a feeling of despair. Or hopelessness. I don't know. I'd never felt anything quite like it before. I thought about Dad and his heart attack. Would he die and leave me an orphan? And what would become of me if that happened? And Norman—what was he doing right now at Camp Weechiwatchi? Would he find some girl he liked better than he did me?

Peter wasn't saying anything, either. He had a sad, lost expression on his face. He looked as bad as I felt.

Pulling myself together I grabbed his arm and said, "We'd better get moving, Peter. We still have all that stuff to carry in from the van."

He seemed to snap out of his trance. He shivered again and looked over his shoulder as we moved toward the door. "I don't like this room, Marnie," he said in a thin, plaintive voice. "It's kind of gloomy or something."

"Yeah," I agreed. "I don't like it, either. Maybe it doesn't get any sun and it stays cold and damp all the time. Maybe that's why they keep it closed up."

And yet I was sure that wasn't what was wrong with the room. So what was it, then? Why was I feeling so weird? All I knew was that I had to get out of there. Right away!

That's when we heard it.

A heavy, shuffling sound from below, like someone dragging a bad leg. *Thump. Shuffle, shuffle. Thump.*

Someone—or some*thing*—was in the house.

And it was coming up the stairs.

4

Peter went out into the hall. I followed him so closely that I was practically riding piggyback.

"Who . . . who's there?" he called.

No reply. Peter called again, louder this time, "Who's there?"

Still no answer.

We tiptoed over to the railing and looked down.

A stocky, middle-aged woman was dragging a loaded laundry basket up the stairs. It was slow going. She was bending over the step behind her, tugging on the basket, so she didn't see us up there, watching her. She was making quite a racket, too, with all that thumping.

A feeling of relief washed over me. I realized then that I was shaking. "Mrs. Gleason—is that *you?*" I called.

"*Eeeeeek!*" she screamed, letting go of the basket, which immediately went bumping down to the bottom of the stairs.

"It's just me—Marnie McKay," I shouted down, "and . . . uh . . . my cousin, Peter. You know, the summer renters."

Mrs. Gleason clapped a hand over her heart

and staggered back against the banister. "Mercy! I didn't know you were here already. I parked on the side and came in through the garden, so I didn't see your car. You nearly scared me to death. For a minute I thought . . ." She broke off and started down the steps in pursuit of the basket.

"Wait, I'll get that for you," Peter called, hurrying down the stairs. "It looks heavy. What's in it, anyway?"

Mrs. Gleason paused to straighten the waistband of her skirt and brush back her wiry gray hair. "They're the sheets for your beds and the towels from the linen closet. They were musty and needed a good wash. I had to do them at home. The electricity's out again here."

Peter picked up the laundry basket and hauled it back up the stairs. "We noticed the light switches didn't work," he said. "We thought the electricity hadn't been turned on yet."

"It'll be on again soon", Mrs. Gleason assured us, following him. "We had a storm last night and it knocked down a couple of lines. Stoneycraig is always hit hardest, being out here on the cliff like it is."

In no time at all, with us helping, fresh sheets were on the beds, clean towels were in all the bathrooms, and Mrs. Gleason had us in the kitchen drinking hot cocoa.

"I'm sorry I wasn't here when you came," she apologized, stirring her cocoa vigorously and tapping her spoon on the edge of the mug. "Like I said, I came over earlier and cleaned up, but then I had to go home to do the laundry and check on Little Orvie."

Little Orvie? Mrs. Gleason seemed too old to have a small child. Maybe he was a grandchild.

"You could have brought Little Orvie here, Mrs. Gleason," I told her. "Peter and I like children."

Mrs. Gleason laughed. "Bless your heart. My Little Orvie's a grown man. Why, he's nearly thirty-two years old. We call him Little Orvie because my husband is Big Orvie. It would get confusing if we called them both just plain Orvie, wouldn't it?"

Then the smile left her face and she leaned across the table. "But maybe you're right. I guess Little Orvie *is* a child. In his head, anyway. He's not quite . . . right, you know."

Neither Peter nor I knew what to say in reply. There was an awkward pause and then Mrs. Gleason hurried on—more, I think, to put us at ease than to explain.

"It happened when Little Orvie was born. A birth injury, Dr. Bartlett told us. There's nothing anyone could have done. At least not in those days."

"I . . . I'm sorry," I said.

Mrs. Gleason waved away my sympathy. "Don't be sorry, dearie. That's the way it is and we've accepted it. Besides, Little Orvie's a good boy. He's never given us any trouble, which is more than I can say about a lot of people's children."

She picked up her cocoa mug and took a long swallow. "It's just that you have to be there for him all the time. And I do worry what will happen to him when Big Orvie and I . . . Well, that will all work out, I'm sure."

"Who's taking care of him now?" I asked.

Mrs. Gleason glanced at her watch and rose, wiping her mouth hurriedly with a paper napkin. "Nobody, that's the problem. Big Orvie's retired, and he usually watches him while I work, but he's down sick today, so I can't stay very long."

She took her mug over to the sink and ran water in it. "I'll be back later to cook your supper."

"That's okay, Mrs. Gleason," Peter told her. "I can do that. I like to cook."

Mrs. Gleason looked at him like he'd just sprouted a second head. "Imagine that!" she said. "A boy your age cooking!"

"A lot of us can," Peter said defensively. "I mean, there are a lot of male chefs on TV who show you how. It's not all that hard!"

"So what time will you be back, Mrs. Gleason?" I interrupted. I didn't want Peter to start in on a men-make-the-best-chefs thing.

"If you don't need me for supper, I won't be back at all," Mrs. Gleason said. "Just leave the dishes in the sink and I'll wash up tomorrow morning."

"Wait a minute," I protested. "Dad said you'd be living here."

"Me? Live here? How could I?" Mrs. Gleason asked. "Not with my two Orvies to take care of."

"But Mr. Maltravers said he hired a live-in housekeeper."

Mrs. Gleason snorted. "That Bill Maltravers will say just about anything to rent this place. He knows perfectly well that I'm no live-in."

"But—" said Peter.

Mrs. Gleason shook her head in annoyance. "I've worked here for a lot of summer renters, but I've never stayed in the house after dark. Never. And," she added mysteriously, "you won't find many around here who will."

"Why?" I demanded.

"Because I have to go home at night to my Orvies, that's why," Mrs. Gleason snapped. She looked sideways at Peter. "They can't cook. They don't have time to watch all those fancy men chefs on TV."

"Hey—" Peter began.

"What I meant, Mrs. Gleason," I said, cutting Peter off again, "was why won't anyone else from Pedlar's Green stay here after dark?"

Mrs. Gleason shrugged. "Old houses make a lot of creaky noises. Some renters have used that as an excuse to move out without paying the rent. That's why Stoneycraig's gotten a bad name."

"*A bad name?*" I demanded. My voice came out so high-pitched that I was afraid half the dogs in the county would come running. "You're leaving us alone tonight in a house that has a bad name?"

Mrs. Gleason held up her hands.

"Do you really think I'd leave you two dear children alone in this place if I thought there was anything wrong with it?" she accused. "Boards creak in old houses. And Stoneycraig is built on a cliff. There are caves in the rocks. When the wind blows, there's an echo."

She looked at us sharply. "But if you're afraid to be alone, I'll stay."

"What do you think, Peter?" I asked.

"I think we'll do just fine on our own," he snapped. I could tell he was still miffed at Mrs. Gleason for her crack about fancy men chefs.

"Good," Mrs. Gleason said briskly. "Now let me get a couple of kerosene lamps from the pantry and I'll show you how to light them. If the electricity doesn't come back on, you'll need them tonight."

"I know how to light a kerosene lamp," Peter said. "So does Marnie."

"Good," Mrs. Gleason said again, nodding her approval. "I'll get you some matches, too. There are candlesticks on just about every table in the house."

She looked out the kitchen window. "It gets dark early on these overcast days. And I think another storm is coming."

Mrs. Gleason was right. We did get another storm.

After she left, Peter and I carried in all the suitcases and boxes from the minivan. I'd brought a lot with me, since I'd be here all summer, and Peter didn't want to leave his out in the van, because the roof had sprouted a mysterious leak.

It was beginning to rain when we finally finished carrying everything upstairs. It was a thin, misty drizzle, the kind of rain that makes you feel more clammy than wet.

They'd had a late spring up here, so it was unusually cool for June. The house was cold and damp. I guessed it would take a long time and a lot of sun to warm up those thick stone walls.

Mrs. Gleason had laid wood and kindling in all the fireplaces, but somehow neither Peter nor I wanted to light them. If we did, we'd either have to sit upstairs in our bedrooms or in the living room with its stiff, antique furniture. There was no family room. The kitchen was just about as informal as this house got.

Sitting there later in the padded rocking chair by the huge old fireplace, my feet propped up on a footstool, I understood why, in the old days, people didn't need dens and family rooms. This one was furnished for comfort. Even the chairs along the scrubbed pine table had cushions on both seats and backs. And the floor-to-ceiling cupboard with its twinkling dishes and pewter made the room look cheerful and cozy.

It had stopped drizzling, but the sky was growing darker, even though it was still afternoon. We'd lit both the kerosene lamps, and they cast flickering shadows on the walls.

"I think Mrs. Gleason's storm is coming," I said, getting up from the rocker and looking out the window. "It looks like a big one, too."

Peter grunted absentmindedly. He was busily chopping green onions for what he called his Gumboburger Delight. "I want to get this thing going," he said. "It has to simmer a long time so the flavors marry."

Marry was obviously another one of his new cooking terms. I'd never heard of food being married before, but figured I'd better not admit it.

Away in the distance I heard the first, faint rumble of thunder.

Peter laid down the chopping knife and browned

the hamburger in a large cast-iron frying pan he'd found somewhere. Then he threw in the onions, a can of drained mushrooms, the chicken gumbo soup and some diced Mexican Velveeta. He stirred everything together and sniffed at it, puckering his forehead thoughtfully.

"Excellent," he finally pronounced, clapping a cover on the pan and turning down the gas burner with a flourish. "We'll just let that simmer until suppertime."

"The smell is to die for," I said. My stomach growled. "It's making me starving-to-death hungry!"

Peter blushed with pleasure.

"It's nothing, really," he said modestly. "Just a little something I dreamed up." He seemed quite proud of himself.

We ate early. There wasn't much else to do. We kept expecting the full force of the storm at any moment, but it was still out there at sea, rumbling ominously. It was coming, though, we could tell. It seemed to be moving in closer.

The gumboburgers were incredible. Peter served them on toasted sesame buns with a Caesar salad on the side.

The electricity was definitely down for the count. We ate by lamplight. I'd also lit a couple of candles and placed them on the center of the table. It would have been a romantic setting if it had been anyone but the two of us.

"You're wearing your hair longer now," Peter said, looking up from his salad. "It's way down past your shoulders."

I shrugged helplessly. "I figured if it was longer,

the weight of it might pull some of the curl out. I hate my hair!"

Peter squinted at me thoughtfully. "You know, Marnie, your hair isn't as bad as you think. There was this old painting in the library at Ecclecleuch. It was done by some famous artist and was supposed to be worth a lot. It was of a medieval woman—a queen, I think—standing by the window of a castle, looking out."

He looked down, suddenly shy. "Anyway, her hair was a lot like yours. You know, red and curly and kind of wild, except hers was longer. It hung all the way down her back. I used to look at that picture a lot because it reminded me of you. I'd wonder what you were doing."

"Why, Peter," I said in amazement. "That's the nicest thing you ever—"

The phone rang. It was Dad, calling to make sure we were okay.

I managed to answer his questions about Mrs. Gleason without telling him she wouldn't be staying with us at night. Peter and I had decided on that ahead of time. The doctor had told me how important it was that Dad not be worried or stressed, and I didn't want him to get worked up about Mr. Maltravers's mistake. It wouldn't do any good, anyway.

The storm finally hit when I was writing a letter to Norman, trying to give him the impression that Pedlar's Green was swarming with college boys from Harvard and Yale, home for the summer and looking for love. Peter was reading the latest issue of his *Lacrosse* magazine.

A crash of thunder accompanied the first flash of lightning. No time to count the seconds between. It was close. Really close. A few more flashes and a few more booms and then the rains came.

I was glad Peter was here with me. It would have been scary to sit this storm out by myself. In the beginning, when Dad and I made plans to come to Stoneycraig, we figured I'd take the train up and spend the first week with just Mrs. Gleason for company. Peter's deciding to drive up with me made everything easier—especially, as it turned out, weathering a thunderstorm in a big old house.

Another crack of thunder.

Alone with Peter . . . I hadn't really thought of it that way before. I know Dad would have had a fit if I'd been up here alone with Norman. But Peter? No, he didn't count. I mean, we'd practically lived in each other's houses ever since we were in diapers. This was nothing new. Besides, it was too late now for us to start worrying about getting a chaperone. The rain had begun to come down in buckets.

I went to bed early. It had been a long day, and, tell you the truth, during a thunderstorm I always feel safer when I'm huddled under a pile of blankets.

I woke up after midnight. The storm had passed. It was silent. Dead silent.

It must have been the total silence after the wind and the rain that awakened me.

And it seemed cold in my room—an indescribable, bone-numbing cold, as if the warmth were being sucked out of my body.

The sky was cloudless now and the moon was

full and shone eerily in through the window beside my bed.

The sobbing, when it came, was distant and faint. I sat up in bed and listened. Was it Peter, having a nightmare?

No, that wasn't Peter.

It was a woman. A woman weeping as if her heart were breaking.

5

The sobs grew louder. Closer. Great, gasping sobs.
Sobs that seemed to come from all around, bouncing off the walls and echoing up the broad stairwell.

I slipped out of bed and tiptoed over to the open doorway.

The bright yellow moonlight flooded in through the arched window of the landing. On the ceiling, pale reflections of the sea wavered and danced.

And then someone moved in the shadows beside me. Someone holding a long, threatening weapon.

I was so frightened that for a moment my heart nearly stopped beating.

"Marnie? Are you okay?" Peter whispered, shifting his lacrosse stick to his other hand.

"Peter!" My breath came whooshing out of me as I grabbed his arm. "You scared me to death!"

"Sssh!" he cautioned. "Listen!"

The sobs came at us again, sobs that ended in

low moans, making them sound even more heartbroken than before.

Suddenly I experienced that same terrible feeling
of hopelessness and despair I'd had earlier in the
music room. The feeling that everything was
wrong, and that I was powerless to do anything
about it.

Beside me, I could feel Peter trembling violently.

I tried to move, to draw him back into the safety
of my room, but I couldn't. My feet were frozen to
the floor.

In spite of the cold, a clammy sweat broke out
over my body, and I was afraid I might faint. I bit
my lip until it was numb and clung to Peter.

The weeping continued, wave after wave of it,
surrounding us on all sides.

Finally a cloud passed before the moon. The
landing darkened and the patterns on the ceiling
disappeared.

The sobbing died. Then we heard, in the sudden
stillness, the grandfather clock down in the foyer
strike one.

We waited, barely breathing, for the weeping to
begin again.

Silence.

The moon broke through the clouds again, but
the house was quiet. Eerily quiet.

"She . . . it's gone," Peter said.

The two of us sat in my room, huddled in the wing
chairs before the fireplace. There were candles on
the bedside tables and on the bureau, and I'd lit
them all.

"I can't stay in this place another night, Peter," I finally said, shivering. "I've never been so frightened in all my life."

"Shut up, Marnie," he snapped. "I'm trying to figure this out."

"So what's to figure?" I demanded. "Peter, we just saw a ghost."

He turned and looked at me. "We didn't *see* anything, Marnie."

"You know what I mean," I told him. "We heard one. That's the same as seeing one."

"Okay, we *thought* we heard a ghost, then."

"What do you mean—*thought?* Are you deaf, Peter, or are you just plain crazy? We heard a ghost. We heard a ghost crying and sobbing. The only thing we didn't hear was somebody rattling chains and yelling for a missing head!"

"Calm down, Marnie," Peter said soothingly.

"Don't tell me to calm down," I said shrilly. "First you tell me to shut up and then you tell me to calm down. I hate it when you do your John Wayne thing!"

"I'm only trying to work this thing out logically," Peter replied. "First of all, we both know there's no such thing as a ghost—"

"Speak for yourself," I said, breathing rapidly. "I've just become a believer."

"Wait a minute," Peter commanded. "Let's try to use our heads. Didn't Mrs. Gleason say that this house makes some real strange noises sometimes?"

I nodded. "She sure got that one right."

"And didn't she also say that there are caves in the cliff under Stoneycraig?"

"So?" I demanded.

"So we just had a storm," Peter said. "A big storm. The wind was blowing full force when we went to bed, wasn't it?"

"What's that got to do with the caves?"

"Everything." Peter said. "That's what a wind instrument is, basically—air blowing into a pipe of some sort, right?"

"Yeah," I agreed. "But—"

"So maybe what we heard was the wind blowing through the caves, and the sound was coming up through the house. Remember how the sobbing seemed to be coming from all around?"

I gave that one some thought. Then I said, "The storm was over, though, when we heard the sobbing."

"Yes, the storm was over, Marnie, but maybe the wind was still blowing down there on the beach. Maybe it just needs to hit the rocks a certain way to make that sound."

"The sobbing stopped when the clouds blew in front of the moon," I said slowly, trying to remember all the details. "Would that mean anything?"

Peter chewed on his thumbnail for a moment before replying. "It could. Those clouds could have been blown by the last bit of wind. So maybe it wasn't a coincidence. Maybe it meant that the wind had stopped gusting."

I was beginning to feel better already. Peter was right. There's always a logical explanation for everything. Well, almost always.

"It sounded so real, though," I said.

"Remember the summer our folks took us to

that ranch in Texas?" Peter asked. "And remember how the wind came whistling down across the plain? It sounded like someone shrieking, didn't it?"

"Oh yes, I remember that," I admitted. "It was terrible. It sounded like a bunch of banshees were after us."

"Well, there you have it, then," Peter said. He stood up and stretched. "The wind can make some very human-sounding noises, can't it? And Mrs. Gleason says a lot of renters have heard weird sounds in this house, too. It's probably been the wind every time."

Suddenly it all made sense. Of course. How could I have been so dumb?

"Peter," I said admiringly, "I'm impressed, really impressed with the way you figured this out. I didn't think about that wind-in-the-cave stuff when I heard those moans and sobs. I thought it was a ghost and I was absolutely terrified."

"It sounded like something from the grave to me, too," Peter admitted. "And I was just as scared as you were. Who wouldn't be? It wasn't until I was sitting here, thinking it through, that I realized what had made that sound."

"You're a jewel, Peter, a real jewel," I said as he went off to his room.

He turned around in the doorway and grinned. "I know. A diamond in the rough."

The sun was streaming in through the window when I awoke the next morning. I could hear Peter singing and splashing in the shower at one end of the hall. I could even smell coffee from down in the kitchen. Mrs. Gleason must have come in early.

Everything seemed so cheerful. So normal.

At first I wondered if I had only imagined last night, but when I looked around the room and saw all the half-burned candles, I knew it had been real.

Suddenly a quote popped into my head. I think it's from the Bible: *Weeping may endure for a night, but joy comes in the morning.*

It seemed appropriate, considering all the weeping that had gone on in Stoneycraig last night!

I jumped out of bed, feeling pretty good, and threw on a pair of khakis and a red long-sleeved T-shirt. After a quick scrub in the bathroom at the other end of the hall, I went downstairs to breakfast.

Peter was already at the table, his hair still damp from the shower and his skin scrubbed and shiny. He was happily digging into a pile of scrambled eggs.

Mrs. Gleason had laid on quite a breakfast. She'd even baked biscuits. And from scratch, too. They were all puffy and golden. The ones you get in tubes never look like that. This summer was going to be a spoiler.

"That was quite a storm we had last night, wasn't it?" she commented, setting a platter of hash brown potatoes on the table.

Peter and I exchanged quick glances. No way would I ever tell her about those weird noises we'd heard last night. Peter wouldn't either. I was sure about that. Neither of us would ever admit we were dumb enough to mistake the wind for a wailing ghost. Wouldn't *that* give the Pedlar's Green locals something to gossip about, though!

"We went to bed early," I said cautiously, my eyes on my plate. "It was raining buckets when I blew out my candle. The electricity is still out this morning, I see."

I didn't say anything more about the storm. I waited to see if Mrs. Gleason would ask us if we heard anything unusual, or were frightened to be alone in the house, but she didn't. She did give both of us a sharp look, though. We must have looked okay to her, because she started talking about the terrible state of the local electricity.

"And the storm last night did more damage to the lines," she concluded, shaking her head. "I hope it's not going to be like this all summer. Big Orvie really misses his TV programs when the electricity's out."

"How's your husband feeling this morning?" I asked, thoroughly enjoying my breakfast. The hash browns were perfect. Brown and crunchy on the outside and soft inside. The biscuits were incredible, too, especially with Mrs. Gleason's homemade strawberry jam.

"He's much better today," she told us. "At least he's feeling good enough to keep an eye on Little Orvie for me."

"You know, Mrs. Gleason," Peter said, "you can bring Little Orvie here anytime you want. He wouldn't be any trouble."

Mrs. Gleason was at the sink, scrubbing the frying pan. She rinsed it and turned to us, wiping her hands on a tea towel.

"Maybe I'd better tell you this right off, so you can decide whether or not you want Little Orvie here," she said, her face sober. "Stoneycraig seems to have a peculiar effect on him."

Peter frowned. "What do you mean? Why should this house have a . . . a peculiar effect on Little Orvie?"

She came over to the table and sat down, still wiping her hands. "He acts kind of nervous and antsy, if you know what I mean. Skittish. He walks around and peeks in rooms, like he's looking for something and scared he's going to find it. Sometimes he won't even come in. He just stands out there in the yard and looks in through the window. I was afraid you wouldn't want him around. He can be a real nuisance."

"Please bring him any time," I urged. "He won't be a nuisance. But why does he act so nervous here? Hasn't he ever told you what bothers him?"

"No. You see, Little Orvie can't talk," Mrs. Gleason explained in a soft voice. "At least not so's you can understand him. He just makes noises. Like a baby trying to talk. That's how it's always been with him."

Her normally cheerful face drooped. Unhappy lines formed at the corners of her eyes and mouth. She folded the tea towel carefully, creasing the folds with her thumb. "He used to be so happy here, too. It was one of his favorite places. But that was when Miss Ellen was alive."

"You mean—Ellen Hadley?" I asked.

"Yes. Ellen Hadley. Of course, she was Mrs. D'Amato then," Mrs. Gleason explained. "I used to come to Stoneycraig a couple of times a week to help out. Little Orvie was ever so fond of her. He'd talk to her in that funny way of his and she seemed to understand. Or at least she pretended she did, just to make him feel good."

"Maybe it bothers him that Ellen—Mrs. D'Amato—is gone," Peter suggested. "Do you think he's looking for her when he walks around, looking into rooms?"

"Yes," Mrs. Gleason agreed. "That's probably it. He was one of the last to see her alive, you know. He'd been over to visit her the day that . . . well, that it happened."

"You mean, when Ellen died?" I asked. In spite of the warmth from the stove, I suddenly felt cold.

Mrs. Gleason nodded.

"Wait a minute," Peter interrupted. "Mr. Maltravers told us that Ellen didn't die in this house. I asked him."

Mrs. Gleason looked first at Peter and then at me. She seemed surprised at Peter's question. "No, of course Ellen didn't die *in* the house. She died out there, on the cliff. That's where she jumped."

I gasped and pressed my knuckles to my mouth.

Peter's face turned a chalky white. Every freckle on the bridge of his nose stood out like a polka dot. "She *jumped?*" he repeated blankly.

"Yes, jumped." Mrs. Gleason repeated. "Didn't you know? Ellen Hadley committed suicide."

After breakfast, Peter and I decided to walk down to the village along the cliffside path. We needed to get out of the house, especially after Mrs. Gleason dropped her bombshell about Ellen Hadley's suicide.

People commit suicide. I know that. You read about it all the time in the papers. And yet you never figure it's going to happen—literally!—in your own backyard.

The path began at the edge of the cliff, by the twisted tree, the one that looked like a hangman's gallows. We could see a small patch of rocky beach far below. A long, steep series of rickety wooden steps set into the cliffside led down to it.

"This must have been where she jumped," I said, gesturing to the tree. "There, where the tree leans out over the rocks."

I walked cautiously over to the edge and looked down. At the bottom of the cliff, lining the beach,

was a row of tall, jagged rocks against which the
ocean was breaking, sending up sprays of foam.
For a moment, in my mind, I could almost see Ellen
Hadley's twisted, lifeless body spread-eagled on
those rocks, being beaten by the incoming waves.

I shuddered.

"It's a terrible place, isn't it?" Peter asked, following my gaze. He took my arm and pulled me
back onto the path that led to Pedlar's Green.
"Imagine what it must have been like for the person who found her."

We started along the path, the wind at our
backs. "Mrs. Gleason said it was the nurse, the one
who was taking care of the baby," I said. "How
awful! Here she—that poor nurse—had gone into
town for just a couple of errands, and when she
came back the baby was crying and Ellen was
nowhere in sight. If it hadn't been for the dog,
down at the edge of the cliff, barking his head off
. . ."

"No wonder Little Orvie acts nervous when he
comes to Stoneycraig," Peter said thoughtfully.
"Maybe he saw her jump."

I stopped walking and stared at Peter. "Don't be
gross. Mrs. Gleason didn't say anything about
that!"

"Why would she?" Peter asked. "Besides, how
would she know for sure? Orvie can't talk."

I could taste the salt spray on my lips, even up
here. I wiped it away with the back of my hand.
"Do you think she ever wonders about it, Peter?"

"Sure. She's his mother, isn't she? She worries a
lot about Little Orvie. You can tell."

"What you're saying, then, is that Mrs. Gleason suspects Orvie knows more about what went on here at Stoneycraig than he's able to tell her. And maybe that's why he acts so weird when he comes here?"

Peter nodded. "Yeah. Could be."

"You know, Peter, I'd like to know a little bit more about Ellen Hadley's suicide, myself," I said thoughtfully.

"I think Mrs. Gleason told us just about everything she knows, didn't she?"

"Maybe not," I argued. "She acted like she didn't want to say too much about either Ellen *or* Stephen. I can see why. She works here off and on. She probably doesn't want to be accused of starting rumors."

"You might be right," Peter agreed. "But what I'd really like to know is why the *inside* of the house spooks Little Orvie. Mrs. Gleason said sometimes he just stands out in the yard, looking in. You'd think it would be the other way around. After all, Ellen committed suicide on the cliff, not in the house."

I stopped walking again and said, "You know, Peter, for the daughter of a top newspaper columnist, I've been pretty dumb."

"What do you mean?"

"What's the first thing Dad does when he investigates a story?" I asked.

"He does research, of course," Peter answered.

"And he starts by going through old newspaper files, right?"

"Okay, Marnie, I see what you mean. You think

we can read up on the suicide in the old issues of the local paper. But does a place like Pedlar's Green even *have* a newspaper?"

"It's got to," I assured him. "Every town has a newspaper, even if it only comes out once a month."

Purple thistles and wildflowers brushed against our legs as we walked toward Pedlar's Green. I wondered if they'd been in bloom the day poor Ellen Hadley leaped to her death.

The office of the *Pedlar's Green Gazette* was squeezed in between Wembley's Drugstore and Miss Mattie's Yarn Shoppe.

We put our cupped hands to the glass and peered inside. It was the smallest newspaper office I'd ever seen, barely wide enough to accommodate a huge desk piled high with papers and a table holding stacks of photos, their edges curling in the sun.

No one was in the office, but the editor must have been in the back room. A door beside the desk stood ajar and I could see someone moving around in there.

I pulled Peter away from the window. "I don't think this is the place to start our research," I told him.

"Yeah, I see what you mean," he replied. "It would be pretty hard to remain anonymous in a newspaper office this size, especially when we ask to see the back issues on Ellen Hadley's suicide. But what about the library? Maybe they keep the microfilm on the shelf and we could—"

"Are you kidding?" I interrupted. "We passed

the library on the way into town. It's just a little
cottage, Peter. One or two rooms of books at the
most. I doubt if they even know microfilm's been
invented."

"And I guess there's no use asking Mr.
Maltravers anything," Peter said, his eyes flashing
indignantly. "He didn't say a word about the suicide, even though I asked him flat-out where Ellen
died."

"Well, he told the truth, didn't he?" I said. "You
asked him if she died *in* the house and he said no.
He wants to get good summer renters for
Stoneycraig. After all, that's how he earns a living.
He must have been afraid we'd back out of the deal
if he told us the suicide story. His first loyalty has
to be to his client, Matt Hadley."

"But what about that Mrs. Gleason business?"
Peter demanded. "He knew darn well she wasn't a
live-in."

"Maybe Dad misunderstood . . ." I began.
Suddenly I had an inspiration. "Of course. Mr.
Maltravers. That's the answer!"

"You've changed your mind? You really think
he'll give us the straight facts?" Peter asked.

"No, probably not. The code of the Realtor and
all that. But he's given me a terrific idea," I
exclaimed.

"Now what?" Peter asked suspiciously. "I hate it
when you get terrific ideas, Marnie."

I dragged Peter over to a sidewalk bench and sat
us both down. "Listen, Peter. Here's the plan. We
do what Mr. Maltravers suggested. We go over to
Mr. Hadley's house and meet his granddaughter."

"Oh no we don't!" Peter said, jumping up. "Are you nuts? Do you really think we're going to go over there and ask that poor girl about her mother's suicide?"

I pulled him back down. "Of course not, dumbhead! We'll only go over there and introduce ourselves, that's all. You know, tell her we're new in town and don't know anybody and that Mr. Maltravers suggested we meet her, so—"

"No!" Peter said, crossing his arms on his chest. "I refuse to be a party to this. It's so dishonest, Marnie."

"No, it's not," I argued. "I'm going to meet Clare sooner or later this summer, anyway. Why not sooner?"

Peter uncrossed his arms and looked at me through narrowed eyes. "So what's this terrific idea thing you're so fired up about?"

"Well," I said, "if we meet Clare, we're bound to meet her grandfather. So we tell him we heard about Stoneycraig's history as a part of the Underground Railroad and would like to know more about it. That ought to get him talking."

"What good will that do? We're still not going to learn anything about Ellen Hadley's suicide."

"No, but we might learn some interesting facts about Stoneycraig, and what's gone on there in the past. And maybe—just maybe—he might say something about Clare's mother."

7

When Clare Hadley opened the door, Peter made an absolute fool of himself.

His eyes bugged out. His jaw dropped open. It was so embarrassing.

Oh no! I thought. *Here it comes. Another one of Peter's big crushes!*

No wonder. Clare was drop-dead gorgeous. Long, straight black hair. Big brown eyes that slanted up slightly at the corners. A smooth olive skin that had obviously never known a living zit.

Since Peter seemed to have lost his voice, it was up to me to do all the talking.

"Hello there," I chirped, "I'm—"

Her eyes lit up. "Oh, I know who you are. Mr. Maltravers told Grandfather and me all about you. You're Marnie, aren't you? Your dad's renting Stoneycraig for the summer. And you"—she turned to Peter, a little dimple flashing briefly in one cheek—"you must be her cousin, Peter."

Peter made a strange sound, sort of a cross between a wheeze and a sigh.

"Yes," I continued. "We were in town and saw your house and . . . well, Mr. Maltravers said we should stop by and meet you."

"I'm glad you did," she said. "Please come in. Grandfather's out doing errands, but he should be home soon. I'm sure he'd like to meet you, too."

There was something shy—unsure, even—in Clare's manner. She spoke in an eager, polite voice and looked up at us from under those long lashes, like a well-trained child who wants to do everything just right. With her looks and—according to Mr. Maltravers—her old family money, I was surprised she didn't act stuck-up or snobby.

She held the door open and smiled at us. Peter wiped his feet like he was about to enter the holy of holies. It's a wonder he didn't take his shoes off. He never wipes his feet when he comes into *my* house.

Clare's house was as beautiful as Stoneycraig, and furnished in the same sort of well-polished antiques.

By now, Peter seemed to have recovered some of his usual cool. He managed to carry on a polite conversation with Clare as she led us down a long hall and into the parlor. I was relieved. For a minute there I'd been afraid I'd have to keep the ball rolling all by myself.

When we entered the dimly lit parlor, I took a step back in surprise, tromping heavily on Peter's foot.

Hanging over the fireplace was a full-length, nearly life-sized portrait of one of the most beautiful women I'd ever seen. Coming upon it suddenly as we had, without warning, startled me. She looked so real. And she was looking toward the door, too, with a welcoming smile on her face, almost as if she'd been waiting for us.

It caught Peter by surprise as well. He stopped talking and stared at it, his eyes wide.

Clare laughed when she saw the expression on our faces. "People always do that when they see the portrait for the first time," she said.

The room was damp and chilly, and a small log fire glowed in the grate. Clare waved us to a couple of fireside chairs and bustled around, switching on table lamps.

"This room faces north," she explained, taking a poker and jabbing at the log. Little glowing sparks flew up toward the chimney, and the log crackled and burst into flame. "It's always colder in here than anywhere else, especially after a storm."

My eyes returned to the portrait. I couldn't help myself. The painted gaze of the woman still seemed to be following me, even though by this time I was seated before the fire. It was uncanny.

"That's my mother," Clare explained. "My grandfather had it painted for her nineteenth birthday. The artist did a good job, he says."

"I figured that's who it was," Peter said, staring up at the smiling face of Ellen Hadley. "You look just like her."

Clare didn't reply. It was hard to tell what she was thinking. Her face was smooth and unreadable.

In the portrait, Ellen was wearing a long white

gown. Her slender shoulders were bare, except for the gauzy shawl she clasped loosely about her. She looked happy. Radiant. Young.

She had no idea what was waiting for her in her future, I thought, and for a brief moment that same feeling of despair and hopelessness I'd had last night on the landing washed over me.

Yes, the resemblance between her and Clare was strong. They had the same features. The same small, straight nose. The same almond-shaped eyes. But the coloring was different. Ellen, with her blue eyes and light brown hair, was as fair as Clare was dark.

Stephen D'Amato, I thought. *That's where the olive skin and brown eyes came from. Stephen D'Amato, the songwriter, who broke Ellen's heart.*

Clare perched on the edge of a straight-backed chair, hands clasped in her lap, ankles neatly together. "I was so glad when Mr. Maltravers said you'd be spending the summer here," she said in that clear, precise voice. "I didn't know what I was going to do here, all by myself."

I remembered what Mr. Maltravers had said about the Pedlar's Green kids working at the summer resorts down the coast. "You mean there isn't *anybody* around here who doesn't leave town for the summer?"

"Not our age, anyway. Whoever's left is either too young or too old. There isn't even a high school within miles of here. I go to a boarding school in Connecticut. I only come home for summers and school holidays."

She looked down and smoothed her short denim

skirt. Her hair drifted in front of her face. It was the kind of hair you see in shampoo ads, long and gleaming. Rippling. I guess that's the word for it. Beside me, Peter uttered a dreamy little sigh.

For some reason, I suddenly felt the urge to give him a good, swift kick. It seemed to me he was getting a little too old for this sort of stuff. How many of these dumb crushes had I nursed him through, anyway? Too many to even count, I decided wearily. Maybe his five months at Ecclecleuch hadn't changed him as much as I'd thought. And *no,* I was not jealous of Clare because of her incredibly perfect hair.

"I've always gone away to school," Clare was saying, "and Grandfather and I usually travel together in the summer, so I've never felt that Pedlar's Green is my home." She glanced up and smiled at us again. "But Grandfather decided to stay here this summer. I was glad to hear there'd be other kids my age at Stoneycraig."

So this is how I'll be spending my summer vacation, I thought. *Clare Hadley and me in the middle of nowhere. And when Peter leaves, I'll have to listen to her carrying on about him. There go my big plans for meeting some cute guys this summer. And there's that rotten Norman living it up at Camp Weechiwatchi with all those hot babes in their bikinis.*

I looked up again at the portrait of Ellen Hadley. Maybe she'd been desperate for a boyfriend, stuck here in Pedlar's Green. Maybe that's why she'd gone overboard for that loser, Stephen D'Amato.

There was something fascinating about that portrait. Especially about the eyes. The way they followed you everywhere. I wondered how the artist did it. I also wondered why Mr. Hadley kept the portrait here, when he'd been so broken up about what Ellen did to herself.

Peter and Clare were talking about her boarding school. He was asking her why her grandfather had picked that particular one.

"I've heard of it," he said. "A friend's sister used to go there. It's very small. And pretty strict, too, my friend said."

"My mother went there," Clare explained, gesturing to the portrait. "I don't know why Grandfather decided to send me there too, though. It wasn't strict enough to keep *her* from messing up her life later."

Peter and I exchanged uneasy glances.

"You know, of course, what happened to my mother," Clare said.

"Yes," Peter answered gently. "We know that she . . . died, after your father . . . you know . . . left."

Clare nodded. "My mother's suicide has been the talk of Pedlar's Green for sixteen years. I was sure someone told you about it the minute you got here."

"Well, not really . . . I mean—" I began.

"That's okay," Clare said, holding up her hands. "I'm used to it. Whenever I come home, something always happens to remind me of it."

She glanced up again at the portrait of her mother, as if trying to see in that calm, painted face the thoughts and emotions of the woman she later became. Bride. Mother. Suicide.

"I was only a couple of months old when it happened," she said. "My father deserted my mother a week before I was born. No farewell note. Nothing. He simply disappeared."

"Look, Clare, you don't have to tell us all this," I protested.

"Why not?" she said, with a shrug. "You're living in Stoneycraig. You might as well hear the whole story."

She got up and poked at the log again. "Anyway," she said, laying down the poker, "my mother was nearly out of her head about it. She kept saying he hadn't left her. And that he'd be back. That he'd never do this to her. To us."

The log shifted in the grate. It looked about done for. Clare laid a new one over the old, positioning it so it would catch what was left of the flame.

"But my father didn't come back," she said in a low voice. "Grandfather said he knew, right from the start, that Stephen D'Amato wasn't worthy of my mother." She shrugged. "He'd always hoped she'd marry one of the local boys. There were a lot of them around in those days. He wanted someone solid and steady, from a fine old family. But Mother went to New York and met my father and that was that."

"I can't believe your father was as bad as your grandfather says," Peter said loyally, in a transparent effort to cheer her up. "Your mother was a beautiful woman. She could have had anybody she wanted."

Clare smiled grimly. "I guess *he* was what she wanted. Grandfather said all he thought about was his music and the songs he wanted to write. I guess he figured that Mother would be a burden to him, once I was born. So he deserted us."

I didn't know what to say. Neither did Peter. My heart was beating slowly, heavily.

"And then she killed herself," Clare said in a flat voice. "The nurse found me crying in my crib. My mother hadn't even bothered to feed me before she killed herself."

She looked at us, her dark, almond-shaped eyes sparkling with tears. "So you see, I was deserted by both my parents. Neither one of them cared anything about me. And the terrible thing is—my being born was the cause of everything that happened."

We invited Clare to Stoneycraig for dinner, but she refused.

Actually, it was her grandfather who refused for her.

Clare had said that Mr. Hadley would be home soon, and that he'd be happy to meet us, but she was right on only one count. He *did* get home early, but he didn't seem all that glad to see us, once he found out we were Stoneycraig's summer renters. It was weird how his attitude changed the minute he found out where we were living. He seemed especially displeased when Clare told him we'd invited her there for dinner.

"Thank you," he said shortly, "but no. I'd prefer that Clare does not visit Stoneycraig."

"But Grandfather," Clare protested, "Why shouldn't I?"

Mr. Hadley glanced up quickly at the portrait of his daughter. "Because all that is behind you now. There's no point in starting it up again."

Mr. Hadley's voice was sharp, but his eyes, when he looked at Clare, were anxious and caring. He was only trying to protect her from her past. Even I could see that. I wondered if Clare knew that her grandfather was doing it out of love.

Maybe not. Maybe it's hard to think of yourself as lovable when you've been deserted by your father and mother, as Clare had been. I figured I'd feel that way too, if I were her. *No wonder she acts so shy and unsure of herself,* I thought.

All things considered, the way things were going, I decided not to ask Mr. Hadley about Stoneycraig's history. I didn't want to set him off again.

"What I can't understand, though," I told Peter later that night as he fixed supper, "is why Mr. Hadley keeps that portrait of Ellen over the fireplace. Why does he do it if he doesn't want to relive the past?"

Peter laid some pork chops in a greased casserole and blanketed them with sliced mushrooms, onions, and green peppers. He said he was doing E Z Neapolitan pork chops. He seemed to have named all his recipes.

Too bad Clare had missed his expert performance as he chopped and diced. He would have loved showing off for her. All he'd done on the walk home was talk about her, how gorgeous she was and what a sad life she led.

Well, at least one of us was headed toward a summer romance. Lucky Peter. I wondered again what Norman, the fink, was up to at Camp Weechiwatchi. Him and his wandering eyes.

"I think I understand why Mr. Hadley wants to

keep that portrait," Peter replied, dumping a couple of cans of Spicy Italian Tomato Soup over the chops and spreading it around with a wooden spoon. "After all, Ellen *was* his daughter, as well as Clare's mother. It wouldn't be right to pretend she never existed."

"But why keep Stoneycraig, then, if he doesn't want Clare to visit it? After all, she's his only family now. She's going to inherit it someday."

Peter sprinkled large handfuls of shredded mozzarella cheese over the sauce. Then he covered the dish with aluminum foil and slid it into the oven.

Closing the oven door, he turned to me, a thoughtful expression on his face. "Maybe Mr. Hadley can't sell the house. Maybe it's one of those white elephant things."

"Oh, he can sell Stoneycraig, all right," Mrs. Gleason interrupted, coming into the kitchen carrying a bucket and a roll of paper towels. She'd spent the day washing windows. I hadn't realized she'd been eavesdropping.

"Mr. Maltravers would like to buy it, but Matt won't let go," she continued, not one bit ashamed of the fact that she'd been listening in. "He's a stubborn old man, that Matt Hadley."

"Why should Mr. Maltravers want to buy Stoneycraig?" I asked. "His family owns half the town already, doesn't it?"

"That's the reason Matt won't sell. The Hadleys and the Maltraverses have been trying to outdo each other for two hundred years. Stoneycraig is the last card in the deck. Matt Hadley isn't about to let go of it."

She opened the oven door and sniffed suspiciously. "What's this you've got cooking in here?" She started to raise the foil for a quick peek, but Peter brushed her hand away and closed the oven.

"Neapolitan pork chops," he said stiffly.

"Neapolitan pork chops?" Mrs. Gleason echoed, raising her eyebrows. She sniffed again. "You mean, you know how to cook fancy foreign food?"

Peter nodded, looking pleased in spite of himself.

Mrs. Gleason gazed at him with new admiration. "Well, if that doesn't beat all!"

I was awakened again that night by the sound of sobbing.

Again it seemed to echo up the stairwell and bounce off the walls. The awful, hollow sound of weeping surrounded me on all sides, coming at me, wave after wave. And then, just when it seemed to fade and die, it would start up again—louder, more urgent, more sorrowful.

I huddled in my bed, trembling, telling myself over and over again that it was only the wind moaning in some cave beneath the rocks. But it wasn't the wind. No matter how hard I tried, I couldn't convince myself that the noise I was hearing had a natural cause.

No, it wasn't the wind. I knew that now.

It was a woman. A weeping woman.

That terrible cold was coming over me again, I realized with a shudder, the cold that seemed to suck the warmth right out of my bones.

In spite of my better sense, I slipped out of bed and went over to the door. A full moon hung over the ocean, just as it had the previous night, but tonight it was behind the clouds. Sticking my hand around the doorjamb, I fumbled for the light switch.

Ah, there it was. I flicked it.

Nothing happened.

Was the electricity really out again, I asked myself, or was She doing it?

A thin ray of light wavered up and down the hall. I gasped and shrank back against the wall. A dark form moved behind the light.

It was only Peter with a flashlight. He was standing just outside his room.

He came over to me, still playing the beam of his flashlight over the hall. Nothing was there. At least, nothing we could see. And yet the sobs kept coming, each one more heartbreaking than the last.

"Is it . . . is it Ellen?" I whispered through frozen lips. "It's a woman, and Ellen committed suicide. Do you think she . . . she's haunting Stoneycraig?"

Beside me in the darkness I felt, rather than saw, Peter shake his head. "No, I don't think so. Ellen didn't die in the house. Suicides are supposed to haunt the spot where they took their lives. Ellen jumped off the cliff."

"So who is it?" I asked. My teeth were chattering so loudly they sounded like castanets.

And then we heard something else.

The piano. The piano in the music room. I recognized the tinny, harpsichord sound of it.

At first we heard only a few tinkling notes, a couple of chords, like a pianist warming up. And then the unseen hands drifted into a song, soft at first, and then louder.

The sobbing ceased. She—it—seemed to be listening.

I recognized the song that was being played. It was one I knew well.

Oh, what was its name?

"My God," Peter murmured hoarsely. "Someone's playing 'Until Forever.'"

Yes, of course. That was what it was! "Until Forever" had swept all the charts back in the eighties. It had won gold records for just about every musician who played or sang it. It was number one on every deejay's list.

It had now graduated to the status of a classic. Even the Boston Pops had an orchestrated version of it, and one of the Metropolitan Opera's leading Italian tenors had made it his signature song.

"Until Forever" was such a beautiful song that it brought tears to your eyes. The words were even more powerful than the melody. They told of a love that would last through all eternity.

And now, at this very minute, Peter and I were hearing that song played by ghostly hands on an antique piano!

The cold got worse. A few minutes before I wouldn't have thought that was possible. Whatever it was that was stealing the warmth from my body had moved in closer. The cold was nearly unbearable.

Something was on this landing! And it was right beside me!

I nearly fainted with fear.

And then it—the somebody or something— drifted away. I could feel it leave my side and float down the hall toward the music room, as if drawn by the music. I felt the blood returning to my body. Beside me, Peter was breathing raggedly. He must have felt it, too.

But wait! What was happening? There was something wrong with the way the song was being played. I knew the melody, and two notes were missing. Over and over again in the refrain, those two notes came up missing. Why?

The ghostly music died with a faint ripple of keys.

The grandfather clock down in the foyer struck one, just as it had last night. Peter and I waited again for the sobbing, but it didn't come. The moon came out from behind the clouds and shone in through the arched window.

"Come on!" said Peter, grabbing my arm. He dragged me down the hall, toward the music room.

"Peter, no!" I cried, but he didn't listen.

Peter pushed the door open and we entered the room.

It was as cold in here as it had been out in the hall. But even worse than the cold was the incredible feeling of despair and unhappiness that rolled over me like a thick, wet fog.

I reached out and, with a trembling hand, groped for the wall switch. This time, the overhead light came on.

The room looked just as it had earlier. With one exception.

The silver candelabra was on the floor, and all the candles were scattered.

I used to wonder why, in thriller movies, the heroines always creep around in the dark investigating strange noises instead of running out of the house, screaming for help. Or why they never tell anybody about it later.

Now I understood. You creep out to see what's going on because you simply have to know, no matter what. And when you find out what's there, you don't tell anyone about it because you'd rather die than have people think you're crazy.

At least, that's how it was with Peter and me. We knew now that what we'd been hearing the past two nights was not the wind or the creaking of an old house.

Stoneycraig was haunted.

But by whom? Or what?

Peter and I sat up half the night trying to figure it out:

Was Ellen Hadley the ghost? Did she roam the

midnight halls of Stoneycraig, mourning her sui-cide? So why wasn't she down by the cliff's edge, then, a ghostly woman in white, fluttering and sobbing beside the hangman's tree?

Or was She, the weeper, someone who'd lived in this house years ago, someone we didn't know any-thing about?

And what about the piano? Who was playing that song? And why would the ghostly piano player choose a hit song like "Until Forever"?

If Ellen Hadley was the ghost, maybe the piano playing was only part of her supernatural sound-track. After all, she had this thing for musicians, didn't she?

Or did a second ghost haunt Stoneycraig?

"One thing's for sure," I told Peter. "It isn't Stephen D'Amato. He's probably a fat, middle-aged woman chaser right now, playing in some tacky piano bar a thousand miles from here. Besides, even if he *is* dead, that kind of guy isn't sensitive enough to be a ghost. Scuzzballs don't haunt houses."

This whole haunting thing sounded unbelievable, even to Peter and me. Even after what we'd just been through. We'd both been brought up never to believe in ghosts or hauntings. Dad always told me things like that were just superstitious nonsense. Dad believed there was a logical explanation for everything.

Dad was wrong. Dead wrong.

If we'd had any sense, we would have cleared out of Stoneycraig the very next morning. Instead, we gave ourselves all kinds of reasons for staying. One was that it probably wouldn't happen again.

"After all," we told each other, "Mrs. Gleason's been working here for years, and she's never heard anything, has she?"

Another reason—the most important one—was that I didn't know how to tell Dad about what had happened. Knowing how he felt about ghosts and goblins and things that go bump in the night, I was afraid he'd think we'd both totally freaked out.

"And then he'll either have another heart attack or never let me out of his sight again," I said. "I don't know which is worse."

So we decided to shut up and hang tight at Stoneycraig.

It seemed like a good idea at the time, anyway.

Mrs. Gleason brought Little Orvie with her in the morning.

Little Orvie was huge. I mean, really huge. Arnold Schwarzenegger huge.

"The flower beds need a good weeding," she told us. "And Little Orvie needs some fresh air."

By the looks of him, Little Orvie got lots of fresh air. It was almost scary to see him out there, pushing a wheelbarrow with one hand and plucking dead bushes from the ground like they were daisies.

And yet there was also something gentle about Little Orvie. He smiled at us when we first met. It was a sweet, almost apologetic smile, as if he felt responsible for his shortcomings, and he said something in his strange, jumbled language that neither Peter nor I could understand.

Little Orvie might have been a handsome man, if things had been different. If he'd stood tall, instead

of slouching, shoulders slumped and head down.
And if he didn't walk in that uncertain, shambling
sort of way.

He had his mother's periwinkle blue eyes, too,
pale against his tanned skin, only his had a blurred,
out-of-focus look, as if he were looking inside himself at things only he could see.

"You have a guest," Mrs. Gleason announced,
brimming with excitement, as Peter and I were fin-
ishing breakfast.

Clare Hadley appeared in the doorway, rosy and
windblown.

Peter leaped to his feet at the sight of her, practically knocking over his chair. I caught it just in
time.

Clare was wearing narrow-legged jeans and a
turtleneck pullover. Her long, straight hair hung
down her back in a glossy sweep. She had that mil-
lion-dollar throwaway chic look most of us would
kill for.

I blinked. Clare looked almost like another person. Yesterday she'd seemed so shy and reserved,
especially around her grandfather. Today she acted
. . . well, liberated, like she'd just been let out of
jail.

"Grandfather's gone for the day," she said happily. "I'm on my own, so I've come to see the
house, if you'll let me."

Peter started to stammer something, so I took
charge.

"But," I protested, "I thought your grandfather
said you weren't supposed to come here."

Clare tossed back her hair in a gesture of defiance. "Maybe it's time I decided what was best for me. After all, I'm"—she glanced quickly at Peter—"sixteen. Old enough to do as I please."

Peter gave her an idiotic, besotted smile in return. *Besotted* was a word I'd learned recently. It means *stupefied, infatuated,* and at this particular moment it fit Peter to a tee. He looked exactly like Dopey in *Snow White.*

Just then, Little Orvie came into the kitchen. His eyes widened when he saw Clare, and he began to babble excitedly, incoherently.

"Orvie," scolded his mother. "Stop this carrying on. You know perfectly well who Clare is."

Little Orvie shrank back against the counter. "Nooo! Nooo!" he said, pointing to Clare. "Gahh! Gahh!"

"What's he saying?" I whispered.

"He's saying 'gone,'" Mrs. Gleason said, frowning. Then her brow cleared. "Oh, I know what's bothering him."

She spoke slowly and distinctly to Orvie. "No, Orvie, this is not Miss Ellen. This is Clare. Clare Hadley, Miss Ellen's little girl."

Orvie stopped making those sounds and stared at Clare.

"He knows Clare," Mrs. Gleason explained over her shoulder, "but he only sees her down in Pedlar's Green. Finding her here, at Stoneycraig, must have been a shock. You see, he knows that Miss Ellen is . . . gone, but Clare looks so much like her mother that . . . "

She patted her son's broad shoulder and sighed. "Oh, Orvie," she said. "Who knows what strange fancies come and go in that poor head of yours."

Clare went up to Orvie and took his hand. "It's just me, Orvie. Clare," she said gently. "You know me, don't you?"

Little Orvie's blue eyes were solemn. "Caa-er," he said.

"Oh, that's nice, Orvie. You can say my name."

"Caa-er," he repeated.

"We're going to see the house, Orvie," Peter said. "Would you like to come, too? You can help. Your mother says you know your way around Stoneycraig."

Orvie nodded hesitantly, even though that look of fear had come back to his face.

We made a strange-looking parade as we wove our way through the house like a four-person conga line.

First came Peter, our fearless leader, playing the genial host. Then Clare, looking wistful. "I was so little the last time I was here," she told us. "I have only the vaguest memories of this house."

I was right behind Clare, followed by Little Orvie, quivery as a bowl of Jell-O, waving his hands and uttering what sounded like laments in that peculiar language of his.

Clare's face grew sadder and longer as we went from room to room. I figured she was probably wishing her mother hadn't committed suicide, and that they were living here now, together and at peace with the past.

Orvie got more agitated as we climbed the stairs. I almost called to Mrs. Gleason to come get him, but thought better of it. It might upset him even more.

Poor Orvie. He'd been so happy at Stoneycraig when Ellen was alive. But now she was dead, and he knew—*what did he know about this old house?*

We stopped, at last, at the door to the music room.

The room was just as Peter and I had left it last night. The door was open and the candelabra was still on the floor.

"This was my father's music room," Clare said softly. "Grandfather was angry that I came in here last time."

She stood in the doorway, looking around for what seemed ages. Finally she said, "I can't believe my father was as bad as Grandfather says he was."

She turned to Peter and me, her eyes huge. "You know, when I was small, I found a letter he'd written to my mother. It was in one of her books. Grandfather caught me reading it and took it away. I think he burned it."

"Did it . . . did it say anything important?" I asked hesitantly.

"It was a love letter," Clare told us. "It was beautiful, really. He didn't sound like a man who would desert his wife and baby."

She walked into the room. Peter and I hovered in the doorway, watching. I didn't feel like going into that room. Not after last night. Peter must have felt the same way, too.

Behind us, Orvie was moaning and wringing his hands.

Clare bent down and picked up the candelabra,

setting it on the piano and replacing the scattered candles. "I remember this candelabra," she said dreamily. "I thought it was so beautiful. It was right here, on the piano."

Suddenly Little Orvie erupted into a series of hoarse screams.

"Baah! Baah!" he shouted, pointing at Clare. He said it over and over again. "Baah! Baah!"

Bad. Was he saying, "bad"?

Or was he simply making sounds?

No, he was saying "bad."

But why was he pointing to Clare when he said it?

10

Little Orvie sure knew how to break up a party.

Mrs. Gleason came running when she heard his screams and hauled him off downstairs to the kitchen.

"I might have known something like this would happen," she said, her mouth a grim line. "He shouldn't come here. Not anymore."

"I . . . I guess I should go, too," Clare said, more to Peter than to me.

"But you just got here," Peter argued.

Clare shook her head. "Poor Orvie. I feel like this is all my fault."

"How could it be?" I demanded. "Mrs. Gleason says he always acts weird when he comes to Stoneycraig."

"But I was the one who caused it this time," Clare said. "My being here reminded him of my mother, and it set him off."

"Anything might have set him off," Peter said. "Please don't go!"

Clare glanced out of the window on the landing. "Uh-oh! It's Mr. Maltravers. That does it. I've really got to leave now."

I followed her gaze. Down below someone was getting out of a red Miata. Someone in a flashy plaid jacket.

"If he knows I'm here, he'll tell my grandfather." The old Clare was back now, the timid, unsure one.

"But why would he do that?" Peter asked. I could tell he was still hoping she'd stay.

She made a face. "Because Grandfather told him he doesn't want me here." She lowered her voice. "Besides, I think he's afraid I'll fall in love with Stoneycraig and talk Grandfather into moving back. Mr. Maltravers wants to buy Stoneycraig, you know."

She glanced out of the window again. "Oh gosh, he's coming to the front door. How am I going to get out of here without him seeing me?"

There was a narrow servant's staircase beside the music room. It led down to the kitchen. "Come on, then," I urged, grabbing her arm. "You can slip out the side door. He won't see you that way. But what about your car?"

"I came on foot along the cliff path," Clare explained breathlessly as we scampered down the stairs. "Nobody saw me."

I resolved to make sure Mrs. Gleason kept Clare's visit a secret. I figured she probably would. Mrs. Gleason was no dummy.

"Wait," Peter said desperately, just before she darted out the side door. "When can I—we—see you again?"

"I'll call," she said, and that little dimple flashed in her cheek. "Grandfather's got a lot of out-of-town business this week."

Mr. Maltravers was talking to Mrs. Gleason in the foyer when Peter and I joined them. They were too intent on what they were saying to pay any attention to us.

Mr. Maltravers seemed angry about something.

"Has Little Orvie been here?" he was asking. "I saw his wheelbarrow by the garden."

Mrs. Gleason put her hands on her hips. "Yes, he was, and he ran like a scared rabbit when he saw you. As usual."

"Haven't I told you to keep Orvie away from Stoneycraig?" Mr. Maltravers demanded.

"Little Orvie's my son," Mrs. Gleason said, her eyes flashing. "I always figured I could bring him to work with me if I wanted to. Unless," she added coldly, "you get lucky and find somebody else who wants this job."

Mr. Maltravers took a step backward and held up his hands. "Whoa!" he said. "Let's not make a big thing of this."

"Maybe we should," Mrs. Gleason snapped. "You've had a bug up your nose about Little Orvie coming to Stoneycraig for years, even when Miss Ellen lived here."

"No, it was only after Stephen left, when Ellen was living alone in this house, that I first told Little Orvie not to come around," Mr. Maltravers corrected. His voice softened, became more wheedling. "Mrs. Gleason, you know as well as I do that Orvie is not responsible for anything he does."

"My Orvie's a good boy," Mrs. Gleason declared. "He wouldn't hurt a fly. Are you saying you think he might have harmed Miss Ellen? Why, he fairly worshipped that woman."

She glared at Mr. Maltravers. "But you know all about that, don't you? You were pretty sweet on her yourself. You and all the other local boys."

"Please, Mrs. Gleason," Mr. Maltravers said, ignoring Mrs. Gleason's last barb. "I'm only thinking of Little Orvie. Yes, he's a good boy, but he *does* get nervous and excitable at times. It's not right for him to hang around Stoneycraig. He still remembers Ellen, and I think he keeps looking for her."

He eyed Mrs. Gleason sternly. "Besides, this *is* a rental property, you know. He scares the tenants when he comes poking around. So I'm asking you again to keep Little Orvie away from Stoneycraig, okay?"

"Actually, I'd already decided to do just that, not that it has anything to do with you," Mrs. Gleason snapped. "I'm doing it for *my* reasons, not yours." She turned on her heel and stomped back to her kitchen.

Mr. Maltravers looked after her, frowning. Then he seemed to see us for the first time.

"Hey, kids!" he exclaimed with a bright, toothy smile. "How's it going?"

"Fine," I said, marveling at his sudden change of mood. "Just fine."

"You settled in okay?"

"Yes." It was Peter's turn this time. "The house is a lot bigger and nicer than we thought it would be."

"No problems then, eh?" Mr. Maltravers asked, eyeing us closely.

"No. Everything's just great," I piped up, crossing my fingers behind my back.

Mr. Maltravers still didn't give up. "It's an old house," he said with a brittle laugh. "You have to get used to all the noises an old house makes."

Peter opened his eyes wide, the very picture of innocent boyhood, and said, "Gosh, Mr. Maltravers. We haven't heard a thing. Why, we think Stoneycraig's totally super!"

That seemed to satisfy Mr. Maltravers. He left soon after.

I wondered briefly if he knew about the ghost.

No, probably not. He wouldn't keep renting this house out if he knew something like that was going on.

I was alone in the kitchen when Dad called that night. It was late, and Peter was in bed.

Again, I managed to convince him that everything was going great and we were enjoying Stoneycraig and Pedlar's Green.

As I hung up the phone, I saw something moving just outside the kitchen window. And then, to my horror, a face appeared, pressed up against the glass.

It was Little Orvie. When he saw me look his way, he disappeared.

My heart was thumping so hard I had to sit down.

What was Orvie doing here? Why was he watching me?

And was he really as harmless as Mrs. Gleason said?

11

"I'm sure Little Orvie meant no harm," Mrs. Gleason told me the next morning.

I'd been waiting. I'd met her at the front door and laid it on her about her son, the Peeping Tom.

"Maybe he meant no harm, Mrs. Gleason, but he nearly scared me to death."

"My Orvie wouldn't hurt a fly," she protested, her lips a thin, tight line.

I'd heard that one before. Maybe Orvie didn't hurt flies, but what did he do to humans? After I'd gotten my wobbly legs moving again last night, I'd dragged Peter out of bed and we'd gone around checking the locks on every door and window in the house.

"What was Orvie doing up here, anyway?" I demanded. "Why is he wandering around late at night? Besides, I thought you were going to tell him never to come here again."

"I was. I did," Mrs. Gleason said. Her mouth

relaxed. I could see now that she'd been holding it tight to keep it from trembling.

She walked into the kitchen, me trailing her like an avenging bloodhound, and sank into a chair.

"It was seeing Clare yesterday, here at Stoneycraig, that did it," she said weakly, staring straight ahead. "Yes, that was it. And it won't happen again, I promise. Little Orvie gets mixed up sometimes. That's all it was. Just one of Orvie's little mix-ups."

Who was she trying to convince, herself or me?

"It won't happen again," she repeated in a stronger voice, turning her head and meeting my eyes straight on. "So do you think we could just forget the whole thing? After all, it's over and done with, and you're none the worse for your scare."

"Well . . . okay," I agreed, nodding. "As long as you make sure Little Orvie never does that to me again."

Peter got up late. He'd gone back to bed after the Little Orvie incident and slept, he said, like a log.

I'd tossed and turned until nearly midnight, listening for the sobbing, listening for the possible sound of Little Orvie's return. I'd finally fallen asleep, that dead sleep that comes when you're overtired.

That's why I don't know if I really heard the piano or dreamed it.

Did I dream that it kept playing "Until Forever" over and over again? It seemed so real. Even those same two notes were missing again this time, just as they'd been the night before.

Funny, though. I didn't hear a peep out of the sobbing ghost. Maybe that proved it was only a dream.

The tide was out that morning, and there was no sign of fog. It was sunny and warm—our first warm day—and the skies were a glorious blue. Peter and I decided it was the perfect time to check out our beach.

A long, steep series of wooden steps zigzagged their way down to the little strip of rocky beach beneath the cliff. The air had a salty, kelpy smell to it, the way beaches always do at low tide. Seaweed floated in dark patches on the water beyond the rocks.

"It's not much of a beach," Peter said critically.

"Well, nobody promised us the French Riviera," I reminded him. "This is Maine, remember?"

"They must get some pretty bad storms up this way," Peter said. "Look at all the stuff the tides have brought in."

The base of the cliff that directly fronted the beach were piled high with rocks and driftwood. Peter squinted up at the top of the cliff, the part with the hangman's tree that leaned out over the beach.

I hated the sight of that ugly, twisted tree. It made me think of cruelty and death and dying.

"The storms have eroded the base of the cliff, too," Peter pointed out. "A lot of that junk's been washed down, as well as in from the sea. No wonder the beach is so narrow."

I tried not to look at the cluster of large, jutting

rocks, like giant sharks' teeth, lying openmouthed below the tip end of the cliff—there, beneath the hangman's tree. They looked hungry. Evil. I tried not to think about Ellen Hadley D'Amato leaping to her death upon them.

I hoped she'd died quickly, without any pain.

I'm usually a beach person, but I doubted if I'd be spending any time down here this summer.

I shivered. In an attempt to change the subject I said, "So how do you suppose the Hadley family smuggled the runaway slaves to Canada from here, Peter? Couldn't they have gotten them out easier from the cove at Pedlar's Green?"

Peter turned slowly around in a circle, squinting his eyes against the bright sunlight, surveying the sea and the beach.

"No, a lot of Northerners didn't approve of what the abolitionists were doing, believe it or not. Stoneycraig was isolated. The Hadleys could hide the fugitives here and nobody would know about it. Then it was just a matter of waiting for the right tidal conditions to smuggle them out by boat."

I closed my eyes, trying to imagine how the fugitives must have felt standing here, trying to picture their emotions, now that they were so close to the end of their journey.

Instead, I saw Ellen Hadley's body broken and bleeding on those sharks' tooth rocks.

"Let's get out of here, Peter," I said. "This place depresses me. All I can think about is Ellen Hadley's suicide."

"Me, too," Peter admitted. "And I keep thinking

about Clare." His voice changed, got kind of goopy-sounding, when he said her name.

I felt a sudden flash of annoyance. "Look, Peter," I snapped. "This is hardly the time for—"

"I keep thinking how terrible it must be for her," Peter continued. "She's had to live with what her mother did, day in and day out, all her life."

I felt instantly ashamed of myself for having such a short fuse about the way Peter was acting about Clare. I liked Clare. What was the matter with me, anyway?

"I'm surprised she doesn't hate her mother for it," I said, trying to make amends. "I mean, the stupid woman ruined Clare's life."

"Clare's not the type to hate anybody," Peter replied loyally.

It was harder going up all those wooden steps to the top of the cliff than it had been coming down. As we climbed, our conversation kept returning, over and over again, to Ellen Hadley and the way she'd died.

"Ellen has to be the ghost," I told Peter, breathing hard as I dragged myself up the last flight of stairs. "Who else could it be, considering that song we heard? I mean, 'Until Forever' would have been popular right around the time Ellen died. Maybe it was one of her favorites."

"But she didn't commit suicide in the house," Peter argued, joining me at the top. "So why isn't she haunting the cliff, over there, by that tree?"

"Who knows?" I told him. "Maybe she does her thing in both places, but I'm sure as heck not coming here at midnight to find out."

"In every ghost story I've read, the unhappy spirits hang around the place where they've suffered the most," Peter said thoughtfully. "So maybe Ellen suffered the most in the house, then, not out here on the cliff."

"Yes, that could be it," I agreed. "It must have wiped her out when her husband deserted her. She probably sat up in her room and cried a lot. Or maybe she'd go into the music room. It was her husband's special place. Maybe she went in there to think about him and what he'd done."

I paused, trying to collect my jumbled thoughts, trying to figure out what was happening. "But why do we hear that song? I've never heard of backup music for a ghost before."

Peter shook his head helplessly. "I wish I knew more about this supernatural stuff. I always thought it was pure fantasy, so I never paid much attention to the stories I read about it."

He looked back over his shoulder at the house. "Are you sure you heard the song again last night, Marnie?"

"I don't know. I might have been dreaming. And yet, those two notes kept coming up missing every time. That's not something I'd dream, is it?"

We were at the top of the steps, looking out over the sea. Today it was a deep, surging green, with little whitecaps running before the wind.

Such a beautiful view. Back home, most people dream about owning oceanfront property. And yet they wouldn't want this one. Not if they knew what had happened here.

"Peter," I said slowly. "That sobbing. And the

music. I wonder how many other people living in Stoneycraig have heard it?"

Peter shrugged. "We'll probably never find out the answer to that one, Marnie. Why?"

"I was just thinking. Maybe Ellen is sorry she committed suicide, and she keeps trying to find someone to help her."

"Help her do what?"

"Help her, you know, rest in peace. Isn't that what unhappy ghosts are supposed to want?"

Peter thought that one over for a long time. Finally he asked, "But how could we do that?"

I cleared my throat. "Maybe Ellen has to be forgiven for what she did before she can . . . go on. And she has to be forgiven by the person she's hurt the most."

"You mean, by Clare?" Peter asked.

I nodded. "Clare's not a happy person, is she? She's lived her whole life feeling abandoned, first by her father's desertion and then by her mother's suicide. Maybe Ellen knows this and wants to help her. That could be what's making her haunt Stoneycraig. Maybe if Clare knew this . . ." My voice trailed away.

Peter looked at me with dawning horror. "Let me get this straight, Marnie. You're not saying you want to tell Clare about her mother's ghost, are you?"

"Yes," I said, squaring my shoulders. "Yes, I am. If Clare knows her mother loves her enough to keep hanging around the old house, crying, it might make a difference to her."

Peter's lips moved, but no sound came out. Finally he said, "What makes you think that?"

"Because I just know, that's why. If *your* mother had committed suicide, wouldn't you feel better if you knew she was sorry she'd done it? And that she was worried about you?"

"Yeah . . . yeah, I guess so," Peter admitted reluctantly. "And in a way it makes sense. Something's keeping Ellen here, that's for sure. And Clare's not happy. That could be what's locking Ellen into some weird kind of time warp."

"So do you want to go see Clare?" I asked, hoping to nail him before he changed his mind. "We could go right now."

"Well . . . all right," Peter said hesitantly. "If you really think it will help. But we'd better figure out the best way to break the news to her. It's not every day a girl finds out her mother's a ghost."

As we turned to go, something made me glance up at Stoneycraig.

Something dark—a shadow, maybe?—moved in one of the upstairs windows. It wasn't Mrs. Gleason. I could see her out sweeping the front porch.

It looked exactly like the shadow that had appeared in one of the upstairs windows of the Polaroid snapshot I'd taken the day we moved in. At the time, I'd thought it was only the way the light hit the glass.

I wasn't so sure about that now.

I blinked, and the shadow disappeared.

Had it really been a shadow, or had it been a ghost—the ghost of Ellen Hadley?

12

Peter was right. It *was* hard to tell Clare that her mother was a ghost and was hanging around the family estate, haunting and sobbing and making room temperatures drop.

"This isn't your idea of a joke, is it?" Clare finally asked, looking from Peter to me and then back again to Peter, like someone at a Ping-Pong match.

"No, of course not, Clare," Peter said earnestly. "We would never joke about something like this."

We were sitting in Clare's parlor, under the picture of her mother. Those painted eyes were following me again.

Was it my imagination or did they seem anxious, pleading?

I took a deep breath and tried again. We'd been going at it for at least half an hour, and we still didn't seem to be getting anywhere. I didn't blame

Clare. I probably would have felt the same way if I'd been in her shoes.

Peter and I had agreed in advance to make as little as possible of the piano-playing thing. We just told Clare that it seemed to be some kind of background music for the hauntings. Who or what was playing that rinky-tink grand piano was something we didn't want to think about right then.

Grandfather Hadley was not home, thank heaven. What was even better was that he was away on an overnight business trip. We didn't have to worry about him barging in on us the way he had last time.

"Listen, Clare," I said in what I hoped was a calm, sensible voice. "I know it sounds crazy, but everything we've told you is the truth. Peter and I have been through two of those awful hauntings and we're not making up what happened."

I shivered, remembering. "At first we were like you. We couldn't believe it was a ghost. We even tried to explain it away. But we know now that something—*someone*—is haunting Stoneycraig, and we think it's your mother."

"My mother . . . haunting Stoneycraig," Clare murmured in a voice of disbelief. "It sounds incredible. Are you really sure about this?"

Peter and I nodded solemnly. Peter even stuck three fingers up in the air like a Boy Scout taking an oath.

"It's got to be her," I told Clare. "That song we heard pretty much dates the ghost to the eighties, and that's when your mother . . . well, you know."

Clare nodded. "When my mother committed

suicide. You can say the word, Marnie. I've heard it often enough."

Peter took over. "Haven't you ever wondered why your grandfather doesn't want you to visit Stoneycraig, Clare?" he asked gently. "Maybe it's not just the unhappy memories. Maybe he senses something there. Something unnatural."

"The ghost has to be your mother," I repeated. "Everything points to that. And we think she won't rest quietly until—"

"Until she knows I forgive her?" Clare asked quietly. "I haven't, you know. I've never been able to forgive her."

She got up from her chair and went over to the fireplace, staring fixedly up at the portrait of her mother. Again I was struck by the amazing resemblance between mother and daughter.

"It was different with my father," Clare went on, almost as if she were talking to herself. "He wasn't much of a bargain, anyway, according to Grandfather. But my mother . . . What kind of a mother leaves her baby?"

She turned and faced us. Her eyes glittered with tears.

"No, I've never forgiven her. What she did was wrong. But maybe I've been too hard on her. After all, she *was* my mother. And she'd been through a rough time. Maybe she was half out of her mind and wasn't responsible for what she did."

She wiped her eyes with the back of her hand. "I never realized she'd be that sorry for committing suicide . . . or that she'd come back from the grave to . . ." She shook her head, her lips trembling. "Oh, I can't imagine such terrible unhappiness!"

"Please, Clare—" I said, starting to snuffle a little myself.

"I want to help my mother find peace. Now. As soon as possible," Clare continued, squaring her shoulders resolutely. "Tell me what I should do."

It was all arranged. Clare would come over for supper and spend the night. We'd sit up and wait for Ellen. If and when the ghost did her sobbing thing, we'd have to play it by ear. We were hoping that if Clare spoke to her, told her she forgave her, it would be all her mother needed.

Maybe.

There wouldn't be any problem about Mrs. Gleason finding Clare at Stoneycraig in the morning. The next day was Saturday, and Mrs. Gleason wasn't coming in. As she'd told us that very first day, her hands on her hips, "I don't work weekends, so don't bother to ask!"

Clare arrived in the late afternoon, carrying a backpack. She seemed nervous.

Peter had been in a real dither about his dinner menu. He'd finally settled on chicken and rice in a cream sauce. "Elegant, but not too presumptuous," he said.

The role of the cream sauce would be played, of course, by a couple of cans of soup—mushroom and cream of chicken.

We'd stopped at Abbott's grocery store on the way home for the ingredients. Peter nearly drove Mr. Abbott crazy, sniffing the chicken to make sure it was fresh and pawing through the mushrooms in the vegetable bin like a pig digging for truffles. He even found fresh asparagus for the green veggie and bought a long, skinny loaf of French bread to round it all out.

It was a sophisticated menu, designed to impress.

Clare arrived in time to see it prepared, and Peter put on quite a show. He did everything with a flourish, making it look harder than it really was.

First he sautéed the boned chicken breasts in butter and set them aside. Then he mixed the soups with a little milk, the mushrooms and some chopped pimento. As a final touch, he threw in a handful of sliced almonds and a little grated Parmesan cheese.

He stirred most of the mixture into the uncooked rice and spread it, like cake batter, in the bottom of the baking dish. Then came the chicken breasts, followed by the rest of the sauce.

After covering the dish tightly with foil, he slid it into the hot oven, nudging the door closed with his hip. "Dinner in an hour," he sang out.

The dinner was so incredible that we almost forgot what we were there for. We ate in the kitchen, and had candlelight and soft music, courtesy of my portable radio. Peter, the romantic fool, had even gone out and picked some wildflowers for a centerpiece.

Too bad the ghost of Ellen Hadley was lurking in the wings, preparing for her big scene.

And too bad that fink, Norman, was off at Camp Weechiwatchi with those girls in their bikinis. He would have made it a foursome.

The adoring looks Clare was giving Peter were probably curling his little pink toes, if I knew Peter.

And then, at sundown, the long wait began. We popped corn. We played cards. We waited. And waited.

Midnight came. Nothing happened.

"Maybe she's not coming tonight," I said, half hoping she wouldn't. Was I really up to all this?

We were in my room. Clare and I were sprawled out across my bed. Peter was half-asleep in the armchair by the fireplace. It was another cold night, and we'd lit the fire. The flames licked and crackled.

It should have been cheerful and cozy, but it wasn't.

Suddenly the table lamps flickered. Once. Twice. Like a warning. Then they blinked out.

My hands were shaking as I lit the candles on the bedside tables and grabbed my flashlight. "She's coming," I told Clare in a voice that was half whisper, half sob. "The lights always go out when *She* comes."

In the candlelight, Clare looked like a ghost herself. Her face was so white it was almost green. She was trembling from head to toe.

The sobbing ghost of Ellen Hadley was coming. No doubt about it.

First came a blast of that terrible, familiar cold, sucking at my very bones. At all our bones. I saw Clare shiver uncontrollably as she stared wildly into the shadows.

Peter was shuddering. He looked like he had palsy. "It . . . it's worse tonight," he said from between chattering teeth.

The cold was in the room, filling every corner, but the sobbing, when it came, was out in the hall.

This time the sound didn't come echoing toward us up the stairs and off the walls. This time it concentrated all its force, all its horror, in one place.

It was there, *out there*, in the hall, waiting for us.

It was more pitiful and heartbroken, too, than it had ever been.

Clare slid off the bed. Her eyes were blank, unseeing. "Mother?" she called faintly. "Mother, is that you?"

As if in response, the weeping grew even louder. Over and over it came — the wailing, the sobbing, the moaning.

Clare moved slowly toward the bedroom door. She clung tightly to the doorframe and peered out.

"Mother?" she called again. "Are you there?"

She stepped into the hall.

Peter and I were right behind her. Peter's hands were on her shoulders.

The sobbing died. It was silent. As silent as the center of a vacuum. A silence so intense that it almost rang.

And then the piano music began. The melody of "Until Forever" rippled and flowed, filling the vacuum. As always, the same two notes were missing in the refrain.

The three of us stared down the hall toward the music room.

And then we saw it.

The cold was visible now. It looked like a crawling mist.

As it came toward us, it began to spiral upward,

taking on a shape. The shape of a woman. A woman in white.

To my horror, I saw hands emerging from the flowing white shroud. And arms. Arms that were outstretched. Not to me. No. To Clare. It came closer. Closer. I could make out the shape of a head. A face. Even the curve of a cheek.

"M-mother?" Clare whispered again.

And fell to the floor in a dead faint.

13

It was as though a thread had snapped, the thread that bound us to the eerie world of Ellen Hadley.

The mist disappeared. The music stopped. That feeling of being in a vacuum was suddenly gone.

The hall was warm again and I could hear the comforting tick-tock of the grandfather clock down in the foyer.

Peter and I dropped to the floor beside Clare.

"Clare! Clare! Wake up!" Peter called frantically.

I took her hands in mine and rubbed them They were cold. As cold as that white, spiraling mist. I couldn't get any warmth back in them.

Was she dead? I tried to take her pulse. Nothing. Was I pressing the wrong spot? I tried again. This time I felt a weak but steady beat.

"Clare!" Peter called again.

"I think she's in shock," I told Peter, trying to remember my Red Cross lifesaving. "We've got to get her to bed and cover her up to keep her warm."

Between us, we got Clare to my bed and heaped the covers over her. She was still deathly pale and hadn't opened her eyes. I watched her closely. Her eyelids didn't even flutter.

I'd never seen anyone in a coma before, and I wondered if this was how it looked.

"Peter," I said in a hoarse whisper. "We need help. Dial nine-one-one."

"They don't have paramedics in Pedlar's Green," Peter said desperately, "but Mrs. Gleason gave me a doctor's number, in case of an emergency."

I kept rubbing Clare's hands and calling her name as Peter thumped down the stairs to the hall phone.

Clare's hands were beginning to warm up a little. Now if that doctor would just hurry up and get here.

"No, Clare's here at Stoneycraig," I heard Peter shouting into the phone. "She's with us. That's right, the summer renters. What's she doing here? I'll explain all that later. Please hurry!"

Dr. Bartlett arrived faster than I'd expected. He was a white-haired man about Matt Hadley's age. His little black bag was scuffed and worn from years of use. He must have made a lot of house calls in his time.

Clare was just coming to when he walked into the room. She acted a little out of it—trembling and crying softly as he examined her. She seemed unable to speak.

I was glad about that. I'd been afraid she might blurt out what had happened.

"It looks like she's had a shock of some kind,"

Dr. Bartlett said, shining a light into Clare's eyes. "I had a case like this last week—an old lady who'd been playing with a Ouija board. Have you kids been up to something I ought to know about?"

"No," I lied. "Nothing."

"I can't see any indications of drug abuse," the doctor said, half to himself.

"No, of course you can't," I snapped. "We don't do drugs. We might be young, but we're not stupid!"

Dr. Bartlett finally finished his exam and pulled the covers up under Clare's chin. "She's okay," he said, patting her shoulder gently. "She only fainted. She seems to have fallen asleep now, though. Let her rest. It's the best thing for her."

He turned and eyed me sternly. "Something frightened her," he said in a low voice. "I've been Clare's doctor since she was a baby, and she's never done this before. What scared her? What's been going on here tonight?"

"Wait a minute," I whispered.

I tiptoed over to the door and beckoned to Peter. He'd been waiting anxiously in the hall while the doctor checked Clare over.

"Clare's okay, Peter," I told him. "She's going to be just fine. She only fainted."

Peter looked relieved. A little color came back into his face. When the doctor wasn't looking, I put a finger to my lips and shook my head slightly, to let Peter know I hadn't said anything about the ghost.

"What I don't understand," Dr. Bartlett said, "is what Clare's doing here. I'm the Hadley's family doctor, and this is the last place I'd expect to find her, considering how her grandfather feels about her visiting Stoneycraig."

"We invited Clare to dinner and she accepted," Peter explained. "She said she hadn't visited Stoneycraig in years and wanted to see it again."

Dr. Bartlett removed his eyeglasses and polished them on his tie. "And I take it dinner wasn't all that Clare got here tonight."

"We were just sitting around afterwards, talking," I said, trying to sound convincing, "and it got late, so we asked her if she wanted to spend the night here instead of driving home. We have plenty of spare bedrooms and her grandfather's out of town and—"

"Aha, I see," Dr. Bartlett said, resetting his glasses on his nose. He stared at me. Hard. I tried to stare back without blinking, but he won. I dropped my gaze and plucked nervously at the bedspread. I've never been a good liar.

"And then something happened to frighten Clare," Dr. Bartlett suggested, still watching me closely. "What was it?"

Peter spoke up. "I'm sure you know, doctor, that Stoneycraig makes a lot of funny noises at night."

Dr. Bartlett waited, alert and listening, like a terrier at a rat hole.

"Those caves in the cliff beneath Stoneycraig make moaning sounds sometimes when the wind blows through them," Peter continued.

"Oh, they do, they do. Yes, they really do," I said, bobbing my head up and down, eager to back up Peter's story. "It's scary. I nearly fainted myself, the first time I heard it."

Dr. Bartlett narrowed his eyes. "And you kids heard something here tonight?"

Peter and I glanced sideways at each other, trying to decide who should do the talking. Peter made a slight gesture toward me, indicating I'd just been elected.

"Well . . . yes, we did," I said slowly, choosing my words carefully. I figured if I mixed a bit of truth in with the lies, he might believe me. "We heard that moaning sound the wind makes under the house. It really did sound like someone crying, Dr. Bartlett. It upset Clare. It was pretty creepy."

"Just before it started, Clare was talking about her mother and the way she died," Peter put in. "Then the wind started up. It was moaning and sobbing. You could hear it all through the house. It scared Clare. She thought it was her mother. That's when she fainted."

Dr. Bartlett snapped his black bag shut and picked up his jacket. "I figured it was something like that. Now maybe you'll see why Matt Hadley doesn't want Clare coming here to Stoneycraig. This house is as unsettling for Clare as it is for Matt."

He shook his head and sighed, "Well, at least you weren't holding a séance or playing around with a Ouija board like old Mrs. Petrie."

"You . . . you won't tell Mr. Hadley about what happened tonight, will you, doctor?" Peter asked. "We'll get Clare home tomorrow morning, before her grandfather gets back from his trip. I wouldn't want him to think we were, well, bad for Clare."

"I'm afraid I'm going to have to tell him, son," Dr. Bartlett replied kindly. "Clare's a minor and he's her guardian. It wouldn't be right if I kept something like this from him."

He looked back at Clare one more time before leaving. "She ought to be okay now, but you'd better stay in the room with her in case she wakes up."

Clare opened her eyes as soon as the doctor left.

"I just pretended to be asleep so Dr. Bartlett wouldn't ask me any questions," she whispered. "I wasn't sure what to tell him."

She sat up in bed and wrapped her arms around her knees. "I'm not even sure what *did* happen. Did you two see what I saw?"

Peter and I nodded solemnly.

"I thought maybe I dreamed it when I fainted. It was terrible. The haunting, I mean. It really *was* my mother, wasn't it?"

"I . . . I think so," Peter said.

"Her face," I said. "I saw it just before you passed out, Clare. I'm sure it was your mother."

Clare put her head down on her arms. When she raised it, her eyes were dry. "I'm sorry I was such a coward. I didn't even have a chance to say anything to her—to tell her I forgave her. Next time—"

"There's not going to be a next time," I told her. "You can't come here again, Clare. It's too dangerous for you. I was afraid you were dead."

"Besides," Peter added miserably, "your grandfather might even forbid you to see me—us—again, after tonight."

"Well, I *will* see you again. I don't care what Grandfather says," Clare declared, gazing deep into his eyes.

They looked just like Romeo and Juliet in the big balcony scene.

There's an old joke: "All the world loves a lover except when you have to sit behind one in a movie." That's how I was feeling.

"Hey, you guys," I said. "How about me going downstairs and making us a nice pot of cocoa? Hot milk is good for the nerves."

I might as well have saved my breath.

"I don't know what I'll do if I can't see you again, Clare," Peter murmured. He sounded pretty desperate.

"Me too," Clare replied breathlessly. "Oh, Peter—"

They went on like that for quite a while. It was downright sickening, actually. This was definitely not the time for the start of a red-hot romance.

"Well, I guess I'll be going downstairs now," I announced in a loud voice from the doorway. "A pot of cocoa, coming right up!"

Neither one of them even looked my way.

I had the cocoa made, the tray all ready to go, and was squirting whipped cream from an aerosol can into the cups when I heard a terrible banging on the front door.

Blam! Blam! Blam!

It sounded like someone was taking a sledge-hammer to it. Then I remembered that Stoneycraig had a cast-iron door knocker instead of a bell.

Blam! Blam! Blam!

Before I even had a chance to go out into the hall, the door was kicked open. Violently.

"Clare!" bellowed the intruder. "Where are you?"

14

It was Grandfather Hadley.

I ran out into the foyer once I was sure the intruder wasn't a blood-crazed ax murderer, although Mr. Hadley could have passed for one at that moment.

He was absolutely furious. His face was red. His eyes blazed. His thick white hair stood up around his head as if it had been hit by lightning and spray-starched.

"You!" he said in a terrible voice, pointing a long, knobbly finger in my direction. "What have you done to my granddaughter?"

"She's u-upstairs," I managed to stammer. "But—"

Grandfather Hadley thundered up the steps, shouting for Clare as he went.

I rushed back into the kitchen and grabbed up the tray, figuring that if I showed up right behind him with three cups of steaming hot cocoa it would make our little get-together seem innocent and cozy.

It didn't help. What also didn't help was the sight of Peter sitting by Clare's bedside, holding her hand.

"What in blazes do you think you're doing?" Grandfather Hadley was yelling as I scampered into the room behind him, cocoa slopping in all directions.

Peter leaped to his feet, blushing furiously.

"Grandfather!" Clare cried, sitting bolt upright. "I thought you were in Bangor!"

"Obviously! My meeting was canceled and I came home early," Mr. Hadley shot back. "And a good thing I did. Dr. Bartlett's phone message was playing on the answering machine when I came through the door."

He gave Peter a withering look and then returned to Clare. "Dr. Bartlett said he'd just returned from Stoneycraig, where he'd found you in a state of collapse."

"Please, Grandfather," Clare protested. "It was nothing. I only fainted."

"It was *nothing?*" Mr. Hadley shouted. "You only *fainted?* And yet Dr. Bartlett was called from his bed in the middle of the night because your friends here said it was an *emergency?*"

"If you'll just let me explain, sir," Peter began.

"Be quiet!" Mr. Hadley snapped. "You wait for my permission to speak."

I set the cocoa tray on one of the end tables. Well, so much for that. Good thing I hadn't made any popcorn to go with it.

"Haven't I told you over and over again, Clare, that I don't want you coming to Stoneycraig?" Mr. Hadley demanded.

"Yes, Grandfather," Clare said. She sat up a little straighter and raised her chin. "But I'm older now, and I think it's time I—"

Mr. Hadley raved on. "This place is a cesspool of bad memories, and you're a high-strung, imaginative girl. Like your mother," he added grimly. "I don't know why I didn't sell Stoneycraig a long time ago."

"I am *not* high-strung, and I'll tell you why you haven't sold Stoneycraig, Grandfather," Clare said, raising her voice. It trembled a little, but that didn't stop her. "You've always been afraid Bill Maltravers would get the better of you, that's why."

"Ha!" Mr. Hadley said bitterly. "Why, I'll have you know—"

He stopped abruptly and eyed Clare more closely. "What made you faint tonight, anyway? You've never done that before."

Peter tried again. "Please, sir, if you'll just let me explain—"

"Shut up!" Mr. Hadley barked. "I'm waiting to hear what Clare has to say."

"I came to dinner here at Stoneycraig," Clare said. "Marnie and Peter were nice enough to invite me, and I wanted to come, so I came." She bobbed her head in a defiant little "so there!" gesture.

Mr. Hadley crossed his arms on his chest and waited.

"And then it got late, and they invited me to

stay overnight. After all, you weren't home, Grandfather."

I could tell she'd been listening to what I'd told Dr. Bartlett. I crossed my fingers and hoped she'd remember all of it, so our stories would match.

She did. Not only did she remember, but she repeated it practically word for word.

"We were just sitting around, the three of us, talking," she continued. "As a matter of fact, we were talking about Mother and . . . and the way she . . . you know, died."

"Why?" interrupted Mr. Hadley, raising his shaggy white eyebrows. "Why would you talk about something like that?"

"Why not?" Clare asked bitterly. "Doesn't everyone?"

I shot her an encouraging little thumbs-up from behind Grandfather's back.

"Anyway," she continued, "you know how Stoneycraig makes strange noises at night."

"Strange noises? What kind of strange noises?" asked Mr. Hadley, instantly alert.

I wondered what he'd heard in this house. Had he, too, heard the sobbing? Was that why he didn't want Clare to come here?

"You know what I mean, Grandfather," Clare said. "Those moaning sounds the wind makes."

Mr. Hadley seemed to relax slightly. "Oh, those."

"Of course, since I'm not allowed to come here," Clare said pointedly, "I'd never heard that awful moaning and sobbing noise before. So I thought it was . . ." Her voice trailed off.

"You thought it was a ghost, I suppose?" said Mr. Hadley, his lip curling scornfully. "And I guess I don't need to ask whose ghost you thought it was."

"No, I guess you don't," Clare said evenly. "Anyway, that's when I fainted."

Mr. Hadley appeared to mull the conversation over for a moment or two. Then he came alive again and smacked the bedside table smartly with the palm of his hand. Candlesticks danced.

"That does it!" he cried. "I'm taking you out of here. Get out of that bed and put your clothes on, child."

Peter spoke up, his cheeks the color of ripe tomatoes. He sounded like somebody's maiden aunt. "Clare has never once, in the course of this evening, removed her clothing, sir."

He glared at Grandfather Hadley, meeting him eyeball for eyeball.

"Keep your shirt on, sonny. That was not an accusation," Mr. Hadley said.

He turned to Clare. "Get up and put your shoes on, then. I trust," he said sarcastically, with a sideways glance at Peter, "that you have removed *them,* at least, during the course of this evening."

Clare crawled out from under the feather quilt and slipped into her loafers. Her clothes were a mass of wrinkles. All 100 percent natural fabrics, of course. What else?

"Grandfather," she said anxiously, " I hope you don't blame Marnie and Peter for any of this."

Mr. Hadley narrowed his eyes at us. "Of course I blame them. They knew perfectly well how I felt

about your visiting Stoneycraig when they invited
you here. They violated," he said self-righteously,
"my trust."

"But, Grandfather—"

"And furthermore," Mr. Hadley declared, one
finger stabbing the air, like Moses announcing the
Ten Commandments, "I forbid you to have anything more to do with them in the future."

Peter gasped.

"Now, wait a minute—" I began.

Mr. Hadley motioned for silence. "I do not want
Clare to have anything to do with you now or in
the future," he repeated pompously. "Nor will I
allow her to set foot in Stoneycraig again. Ever. For
whatever reason."

His voice rose. "Clare has proven to me tonight
that she is emotional and foolish, just like her
mother. I will not make the same mistakes raising
her that I did with Ellen."

He took a firm grip on Clare's arm and began to
drag her from the room. "And what's more," he
said, "I intend to sell this accursed house at my
very earliest opportunity!"

Mr. Hadley was able to move along the hall and
down the stairs at an incredibly fast pace, considering the fact that he was practically towing Clare.

"Peter!" she cried over her shoulder.

"Clare!" Peter said in a pitiful voice, chasing
after them.

"Lay one hand on my granddaughter, young
man," Mr. Hadley bellowed, "and I'll call the
police!"

They'd reached the front door by this time. Mr.

Hadley punctuated his last threat by flinging open the door and then slamming it so hard behind them that the grandfather clock burst into a little flutter of chimes.

Peter and I were right behind the getaway pair. Peter made a grab for the doorknob, but I pulled him away and threw myself in front of it, arms spread-eagled.

"It's no use, Peter," I gasped. "Mr. Hadley holds all the winning cards. Clare's only sixteen and he's her guardian."

Peter thumped the door tragically with his fist.

When I looked at his pale, pathetic face, something inside me snapped and my adrenaline started pumping like a geyser.

I was sick—sick!—of Stoneycraig. And the hauntings. And that mean old grinch, Grandpa Hadley.

But most of all, I was sick of Ellen Hadley D'Amato, the howling haunt, the sobbing specter, the world's wimpiest, weepiest ghost.

"I hate this place!" I shouted, cupping my hands around my mouth so my voice would carry better. "I. Hate. This. Place!"

Peter stopped moaning and peered at me anxiously. "Are you okay, Marnie?"

"No!" I snapped. "I am definitely not okay."

"You aren't having some weird kind of nervous breakdown, are you?" he asked. "Because if you are, I don't think I can deal with it right now."

"No, I don't suppose you can," I shot back. "Not while you're in the middle of one of your dumb crushes."

My adrenaline was still pumping. Hard.

"What do you mean, *dumb crushes?*" Peter demanded.

Pushing Peter aside, I stormed up the stairs.

"W-where are you going?" he called up at me.

"You'll see," I said, from between gritted teeth.

I heard Peter's feet pattering up the stairs behind me. "You're starting to scare me, Marnie. I've never seen you like this before."

I didn't reply.

"Are you sure you're all right?" he quavered.

"No, I am not all right, dumbhead!" I yelled. "How can I be when I'm sharing a haunted house with a guy who's got mush for brains?"

"Hey, wait a minute. That's not fair! Just because you're all worked up about—"

"This stupid house isn't all right, either," I raved on. "And it's all Ellen Hadley's fault. But I'm going to fix that right now."

We'd reached the top of the stairs. I turned and headed toward the music room, Peter scurrying along at my heels like a frightened squirrel.

"Her and her crying and moaning," I raved. "I hate whiners. None of this would have happened if she'd had the guts to stick around and take care of her baby. She's not the first woman who's ever been deserted by the father of her child, you know."

I threw open the door to the music room and snapped on the overhead light. Surprise, surprise, it actually worked! The cold rushed toward me, as usual, but I only laughed scornfully.

"Okay, Ellen," I yelled. "I know you're in here. This is it. Me against you. If I can't shut you up, I can sure as heck tear your dumb old piano apart so we don't have to listen to that soppy love song any more!"

The heavy silver candelabra with its dusty candles was on the floor again. This must have happened last night, during the haunting.

I pulled my foot back and gave it a good hard kick. The candelabra only bounced a little, but the candles flew clear across the room.

Peter gasped.

Marching over to the piano, I grabbed the lid and yanked up on it. Nothing happened, except that I cracked a couple of fingernails. I tried again. Still nothing.

"There must be a hook here somewhere," I mumbled, and patted around the underside of the lid, where it overhung the piano.

Ah, there it was, I could feel it—not a hook but a small sliding bolt. I bent over and examined it. It was old and rusted in place. I tried to slide it open, but it was stuck fast.

Removing a shoe, I gave the bolt a couple of good bashes. There. That did it. Now it would open.

The lid creaked a protest as I raised it and peered down into the piano's dusty interior.

Uh-oh, it might be harder to rip out those strings than I'd figured. I'd probably need pliers. Maybe even wire cutters.

By now my pumping adrenaline had slowed to a weak trickle and my brains were beginning to take over again.

Why was I doing this? Even if I tore out the

strings, would that really stop the ghost song from playing?

And then I saw something wedged in the strings of the piano, something brittle and yellowed with age. I bent over closer for a better look and drew in my breath.

"Peter," I said. "Look at that!"

My finger trembled as I pointed to the physical evidence that someone, or something, had been actually playing this piano. That ghostly hands had been pressing those keys.

"This," I said, my heart pounding, "is why those same two notes always come up silent."

15

A piece of paper—no, a couple of them, folded together and rolled up tightly—were jammed beneath two strings of the piano.

"Look!" I repeated.

Peter edged cautiously toward me. "You're not going to start yelling again or hit me or anything, are you?"

"No, of course not," I replied impatiently. "Don't be so sensitive, Peter."

Peter heaved an exaggerated sigh and rolled his eyes.

I poked my fingers between the strings and carefully drew out the paper. It felt old and fragile. I began to unroll it slowly and gently, so it wouldn't tear.

"What is it?" Peter asked, hanging over my shoulder.

"It's sheet music, I think," I said, dropping the lid back down on the piano and laying the papers flat for a better look, smoothing them with the palm of my hand.

"It's a song, a handwritten song," Peter said. "And it's on that same kind of music paper we found in the drawer."

I bent closer over my find. "This is crazy," I said. "It can't possibly say what I think it does."

"Let me see, Marnie. You're in my light."

I moved over a little. "It's a song, all right," I said. "But look at the title."

"'Until Forever,'" Peter read. He looked up at me, a stunned expression on his face. "Why, that's the ghost song!"

"And that's not all," I pointed out. "There, beneath the title, see?"

"'Words and Melody by Stephen H. D'Amato. May 14, 1981,'" Peter read in a halting voice. "Stephen D'Amato? Clare's father?"

We stared at each other, our eyes wide with disbelief.

"Stephen D'Amato didn't write that," I finally said, shaking my head. "He couldn't have."

We bent over the musical score again. Yes, there was his name, signed in neat, precise handwriting right below the title.

And beneath that was an inscription in that same meticulous script: "This song is dedicated to my beloved wife, Ellen, and to our child who will soon be born."

I straightened up, nearly bumping heads with Peter. "His beloved wife? What a liar! He didn't mean that any more than he believed he actually wrote that song. How could a sleaze like Stephen

D'Amato write something as beautiful as 'Until Forever'?"

Peter stared down at the paper. "No way. He didn't have the talent, from everything we've heard. As popular as that song is, he'd be famous today if he had. Everybody in Pedlar's Green would be talking about it, anyway."

"And that dedication—" I said. "Why would he say all that lovey-dovey stuff when he was planning to desert Ellen and the baby?"

Peter reached out and gingerly touched the brittle page with his forefinger. "Maybe he heard 'Until Forever' somewhere, so he put it on paper and added that fake dedication to make it look like he wrote it."

"And then stuck it down in the piano? That's dumb, Peter. Who did he think was going to see it?"

"No, it doesn't make sense, does it? Okay, so maybe he didn't copy that song. Maybe Ellen did it."

"Ellen?" I echoed. "Ellen wrote the song down and added that phony dedication? Why?"

"Well, she was probably half-crazy when she committed suicide," Peter explained. "Maybe she was pretending that her husband really loved her and that he wrote a song just for her."

"But she'd have to be able to put the notes on paper, with all the little marks, wouldn't she?" I argued. "Nobody's ever said she was a musician. You can't do something like that if you don't know how to write musical scores."

Peter threw out his hands in a helpless gesture.

"Who knows? I was just trying to come up with some possible explanations. But this is getting us nowhere. Besides, aren't we missing the most important thing here?"

"You mean the fact that the ghost—or whatever—plays that song, and here's the sheet music for it, stuck in the piano?" I asked.

"Yeah. And that two keys have always come up silent, and then we find the music jammed between two strings."

I sat down at the piano and tapped the keys—middle C and D—whose strings the music had been under. They came through loud and clear this time. Those were the two notes that had always been missing in the song, the two notes that led the refrain.

"So who's been playing this piano?" Peter asked. "That music didn't come from the twilight zone."

I spun around on the piano bench and faced him. "Do you think it was Ellen?"

Peter shook his head slowly. "No. She was out in the hall tonight, doing her thing. The music was coming from in here. It was someone else. But who—or what?"

I looked over my shoulder fearfully, half expecting to see the Phantom of the Opera crouching behind me. "I don't know, Peter. That's one thing we've never really tried to figure out, isn't it? We've had enough to worry about, just with Ellen."

"Yeah," Peter said, nodding. "But maybe it's time we started thinking about it. Face it, Marnie, we might have more than one ghost here at Stoneycraig."

"Great!" I said bitterly. "All we need is another ghost. Maybe we can fix him up with poor old Ellen."

I got up from the piano and stooped to pick up the candelabra. As I set it back on the piano, I noted again how heavy it was. Then I went around the room, collecting the candles I'd scattered in my earlier rage.

"You know, Peter," I said, "I can't believe we're actually having this conversation. If I'm in the middle of a weird dream, would you please pinch me?"

Peter wasn't listening to me. He was deep in thought. "That sheet music might be a clue to everything that's been happening around here," he muttered, chewing a thumbnail absentmindedly.

"What kind of clue?" I demanded.

"Maybe if we knew more about Stephen D'Amato and the sort of stuff he wrote . . ." he went on, still ignoring me.

"Whoa!" I said. "I hope you don't plan to ask Mr. Hadley about it. He was pretty worked up the last time we saw him. And that"—I consulted my watch—"was less than an hour ago."

Peter sighed. "No, I guess it wouldn't be the smart thing to do right now. Maybe later, when he cools down and will listen to reason . . . about a lot of things." His voice trailed away sadly.

"We could always talk to Mrs. Gleason, though," he said, pulling himself back to earth with a mighty effort. "I mean, about Stephen D'Amato. After all, she worked for him."

"Not Mrs. Gleason!" I said, horrified. "You

know how she likes to gossip. It would be all over Pedlar's Green by tomorrow night."

Peter shot me a dirty look. "Give me a break, Marnie. I'm smarter than that. I wouldn't tell her what's happened with the piano and the hauntings. What I mean is, we can just kind of casually ask her about Stephen and the sort of songs he wrote."

"I still don't see what good that will do," I argued. "Stephen D'Amato definitely did *not* write 'Until Forever'!"

"No, but maybe he knew the person who did. Maybe he copied the music from him and he played it a lot, and she heard it. Or maybe the person who really wrote that song lived here at Stoneycraig sometime in the past. And maybe *that's* the ghost who plays the piano."

I shook my head. "Not good enough. Wait a minute," I said, my imagination heating up and beginning to bubble. "How about this: What if Ellen had an affair with a piano player? Somebody in New York, maybe. And what if that piano player was the guy who wrote 'Until Forever'? And what if Stephen found out about the affair and that's why he left Ellen? And then she felt so awful that—"

"See what I mean?" Peter said. "There are all sorts of possibilities here, Marnie. All we need to do is a little research. I know we can get to the bottom of this."

I narrowed my eyes at him. "Okay. So you want to start with Mrs. Gleason?"

"Yeah," Peter said. "First thing tomorrow. Right after breakfast."

"I've got news for you, Peter. It's already tomorrow."

The grandfather clock downstairs was bonging out three o'clock when we finally called it a day.

As I stood in the doorway to the music room, my hand on the light switch, I suddenly realized that the cold I'd always felt in this room had disappeared. It was actually warm in here now. I also realized that the usual feeling of hopelessness and despair that went with the room had been absent tonight.

And there was something else.

A scent—light, pleasant, outdoorsy. Unmistakably masculine.

Peter had gone downstairs to make sure all the doors were locked and the lights out, so it wasn't him. Besides, it wasn't his scent.

Yet why did it seem so familiar?

I closed my eyes and sniffed. It reminded me of something in my past. But what?

Then I remembered sitting on my father's lap when I was little. He used to wear an aftershave that I loved. They stopped making it long ago, but I could still recognize it, even after all those years.

Strange I should be smelling it here, in this room.

Was I only imagining it? Was I missing my father or something?

Or do ghosts leave pleasant scents behind, just as they do feelings of despair?

Maybe. And I was smelling it, all right. It wasn't my imagination. But what was the name of that aftershave?

Glenheather! That was it. That was the name. I

*could even remember the bottle. It was square and
green with the picture of a Scottish chieftain on the
label.*

Glenheather. Was it a clue? And would it help
Peter and me discover the identity of the second
ghost of Stoneycraig?

16

Mrs. Gleason's house was one of the old white cottages down by the cove.

It looked like the sort of house she would live in. It was small and neat, with flowers in the yard and ruffled tieback curtains at all the windows.

"What are you two doing here?" she asked when she opened the door.

"We came into town for groceries," I said. That was the truth. Well, we *could* use a head of lettuce. I was glad I didn't have to lie. That's all I'd been doing the last couple of days and I didn't like it.

The inside of the house revealed even more of Mrs. Gleason's taste in home decoration. Patterned slipcovers. Old family pictures on the walls. Crocheted runners on the tables.

"More groceries?" Mrs. Gleason asked, tsk-tsking and shaking her head. "What are you two feeding, an army?"

She led us into her kitchen. "Today's my baking day. The bread's just come out of the oven."

Big Orvie wasn't home, but Little Orvie was at the table. A huge red-and-white checked napkin was tucked into his shirtfront and he was eating a slab of warm bread dripping with butter. He smiled shyly at us as we sat down opposite him.

The incredible smell of freshly baked bread made me swallow hard, and when Mrs. Gleason cut us off a couple of crusty, fragrant hunks, Peter and I tore into them like wild animals.

She seemed pleased about that, and wrapped up a loaf for us to take home. "You'll have to eat it fast, though, or it will go stale," she cautioned.

From the way Peter was looking at that bread and squinting thoughtfully, I wondered if he was planning to use it for breakfast tomorrow. Tomorrow was Sunday and Mrs. Gleason wouldn't be coming in. He'd told me he likes to do big Sunday brunches, and that he has this really great version of Welsh rarebit where he lays crisp bacon and poached eggs on thick slices of toast and then smothers them with cheese sauce (alias cheddar cheese soup). I hoped that's what he was thinking, anyway.

Mrs. Gleason was in such a good mood about our reaction to her baking that it was easy to get her talking. And when we worked the conversation around to Stephen D'Amato, she said a few things that surprised us.

First of all, she told us she didn't know anything about the songs he composed.

"He usually worked in the mornings, and that

was when I did up the kitchen and vacuumed downstairs. I didn't work every day, of course. When I did, he'd close his door so I wouldn't disturb him."

"You mean you never heard him play the piano?" I asked incredulously. "I should think you could hear *something,* even through a closed door."

"Oh, I heard him thumping away and doing chords and things, but I didn't pay any attention. I'm tone-deaf, you know. Besides, you can't hear much when you're vacuuming."

Peter and I exchanged dismayed glances. Tone-deaf! That was no help to our research.

She did tell us, though, that she liked Stephen D'Amato. That was the second surprise.

"You liked him?" I asked. "I can't believe anybody liked that sleazebag! How could you?"

"He wasn't a sleazebag," retorted Mrs. Gleason. "Yes, I know that's the popular opinion around here, but it isn't true."

She hung up her tea towel and sat down at the foot of the table. "Stephen D'Amato was always nice to me. And to Little Orvie," she said, lowering her voice and gesturing to him with a jerk of her head. "That made him a nice person as far as I was concerned."

Little Orvie looked up, interested, at the sound of his name.

"It's all right, Orvie," she assured him. "We're just talking."

"If he was so nice, why did he leave his wife?" I demanded. "And why'd he do it when she was in the hospital, having a baby?"

"I don't know the answer to that one," Mrs. Gleason told us. "Maybe it was some kind of emergency."

"It must have been a big one," Peter commented dryly. "So big that he never bothered to come back afterward."

Mrs. Gleason had no answer to that one, either.

"Well, Mr. Hadley says—" I began.

"Yes, I know what Matt Hadley says about his son-in-law," Mrs. Gleason interrupted, holding up her hands and shaking her head. "That man has never liked foreigners. That's why he disapproved of Stephen in the beginning. And then later, of course, he—"

"Foreigners?" Peter echoed. "You mean, he thought Stephen D'Amato was a foreigner because he had an Italian name?"

"No," replied Mrs. Gleason. "Not because of his name, but because Stephen came from New York City. Around here, that's considered being a foreigner. And him being a musician made it even worse."

I had to bite my lip to keep from laughing.

"Besides," Mrs. Gleason went on, "Matt wanted Ellen to marry one of the local boys. Someone whose family went way, way back in this area."

"Somebody like Mr. Maltravers, I suppose." I made a face, remembering all those I-love-me photos in his office of him in his football jersey and the vain way he swept his back hair up over his bald spot. Somehow I couldn't imagine him married to Clare's mother.

"No, not Bill Maltravers," Mrs. Gleason said,

"although Bill was always sweet on Ellen. That's another thing—"

She paused and looked over at Little Orvie, who was beginning to shuffle his feet and act nervous.

I wondered if the mention of Ellen Hadley had done it. Or was it hearing Mr. Maltravers's name? Maybe Orvie remembered peeping in my window the other night, and was afraid Mr. Maltravers would be angry if he found out.

"Go upstairs and wash your face and hands, Orvie," Mrs. Gleason said kindly, speaking slowly and pointing to the stairs. "I swear, you put more butter on your face than you did on your bread."

"That's another thing," Mrs. Gleason continued after Orvie had shuffled out of the room. "Bill Maltravers is as bad as Matt Hadley when it comes to speaking ill of Stephen D'Amato."

She sat back and crossed her arms on her chest. "Pure jealousy, I call it," she said, shaking her head. "Nobody was good enough for Ellen in Bill's eyes. Except himself, of course. He thought she was a real princess."

"But you said Mr. Hadley didn't want Mr. Maltravers to marry Ellen," Peter said. "Why?"

Mrs. Gleason shrugged. "He didn't discourage it exactly, not in so many words, but he made it plain how he felt, if you know what I mean. The Hadleys and the Maltraverses have always been on the outs. It goes way back. They're the two oldest and richest families in town so they've been rivals for at least a hundred years."

"And yet Mr. Hadley lets Mr. Maltravers handle Stoneycraig," Peter said thoughtfully. "Why?"

"Why not?" Mrs. Gleason snorted. "Bill's the only real-estate agent in town. Besides, the Maltravers Bank holds a second mortgage on the house. Matt took a loan on it years ago to fix the place up for Ellen and her new husband—not that either one of them stuck around to enjoy it."

Then she added, half under her breath, "And Bill will be the one to buy the house, if Matt ever decides to sell."

I gave Peter a signal that it was time to leave. Obviously we'd learned everything we could from Mrs. Gleason. Besides, she'd gotten up and was taking another loaf of bread from the oven, and I didn't want to make a pig of myself again.

"That was a shocker, wasn't it?" I asked as we walked back to our minivan. "About Mrs. Gleason liking Stephen D'Amato, I mean."

"Not really," he said. "Not when you realize that the only people we've talked to about Stephen D'Amato are the Hadleys and Mr. Maltravers, and they certainly have reasons not to like Stephen."

"Do you always have to be such a know-it-all, Peter?" I demanded. "Couldn't you just say, 'Yes, it was a shocker, Marnie.'"

"Yes, it was a shocker, Marnie," Peter repeated in this dumb, falsetto voice.

"Don't act smart, Peter," I said. "I'm not in the mood. I'm running on about four hours' sleep, so you'd better watch out."

"You were bad last night, too, even before you got your four hours' sleep," he said in a normal voice. "At the risk of being smacked senseless, dare

I ask what you meant when you said I get dumb crushes on girls?"

I opened the door on my side and crawled in. Peter, of course, did not open it for me. He only does that for his girlfriends. As I snapped my safety belt I said crossly, "You mean to say you have no idea how nerdy you've been acting about girls ever since you hit puberty?"

"*Nerdy?* Me? Like when?"

"Like when you had the mad hots for Debbi Sue Tipton."

That one hit the mark. Peter looked uncomfortable. "You should talk," he said, with a strained laugh. "What about you and Norman the worm?"

"Norman's not a worm. He's . . . I do *not* act nerdy about Norman!"

"Oh yeah?" Peter smirked. "The guy's a jerk, and you're the only girl dim enough to treat him like a love machine."

"Okay," I said, pushing up my sleeves. "If you're going to play dirty, how about you and Francine Beazley?"

"How about Jonathan Detweiller the third?" he retorted, crossing his eyes and waggling his head.

"Bambi Levine!"

"Roger Cassidy!"

I held up one hand. "Wait a minute. This is getting us nowhere. But, while we're on the subject, just out of curiosity, how come you never got a crush on me, Peter?"

"*You?*"

"Yes, me. Some guys find me attractive. On a good hair day."

Peter stared at me thoughtfully, his eyes squinty little slits. "I tried to kiss you once, but you bit me."

"I was only six years old, and, if I remember correctly, you said you wanted to play doctor, you pervert!"

Peter clapped a hand over his heart, miming deep shock. "You do *not* remember correctly. I never suggested playing doctor with you, Marnie. Besides, *you* were the one who got the nurse's kit for Christmas. The only reason I went along with it was because the pills were little candy mints."

"Okay, okay!" I snapped. "Let's just drop it."

"Thank God," Peter said. He looked at me intently. "Are you *sure* you aren't having some weird kind of nervous breakdown?"

I ignored him. "Getting back to this Stephen D'Amato thing—maybe we ought to pay a call on Mr. Maltravers."

To tell you the truth, at that moment, I felt like an absolute fool. Imagine asking Peter why he'd never gotten a crush on me! I must have been out of my mind. Maybe I *was* having some weird kind of nervous breakdown.

There was a moment of silence while Peter mulled this one over. Finally he said, "Okay, I guess we have no choice. But won't it be hard to work the conversation around to Stephen D'Amato without being obvious? Mrs. Gleason says it's kind of a touchy subject with him. How can we do it without tipping our hand?"

"That's exactly what we're going to do," I told him, thinking hard and fast.

"Huh?"

"Maybe we ought to tip our hand, Peter. Maybe it's time we told somebody what's been going on at Stoneycraig."

17

We were in luck. Mr. Maltravers was just opening his office when we arrived. He invited us in, explaining that his secretary had the weekend off.

Good. We needed to be alone. We had a lot of talking to do, and I didn't want her hanging around, eavesdropping.

I'd had a hard time convincing Peter that the time had come to take Mr. Maltravers into our confidence about all the strange things that had been going on at Stoneycraig.

"But I thought we decided we weren't going to tell anybody about the ghost . . . ghosts," he'd protested. "He'll probably think we're crazy."

"I've been thinking about that, Peter. Mr. Maltravers is the agent for Stoneycraig, isn't he? Maybe he suspects there's something weird about the house but he's never said anything because he wants to keep it rented."

"Why keep it rented?" Peter had argued. "If it's

not, Mr. Hadley's more likely to sell it, and that's what Mr. Maltravers wants, isn't it?"

"Yes, but Mr. Hadley's pretty stubborn about selling, so Mr. Maltravers probably figures it's better to keep the place rented for now."

"How can he, with those ghosts hanging around?" Peter asked.

"I've been thinking about that, too," I replied. "From the way everybody acts, Stoneycraig's always been known as an old house that makes funny sounds and where a lot of things have happened. But I bet nobody's seen and heard everything we have, like that Academy Award performance Ellen gave last night."

"Why us, then, Marnie? How come we're the lucky ones?"

"Maybe because we're Clare's age. And because we've made friends with her. Maybe Ellen wants to use us to get to Clare."

"And now you think we should tell Mr. Maltravers everything?" Peter asked incredulously.

"No, not everything. Just a watered-down version of what's been going on. If we get too carried away, he might think we're lying."

"Do you really think he can help us?"

"Face it, Peter, we're not getting anywhere on our own. Mrs. Gleason was no help. And we're in enough trouble already with Mr. Hadley. Who else is there?"

So here we were in Mr. Maltravers's office, once again surrounded by wall-to-wall photos of Mr. Touchdown in some of his finest moments.

Mr. Maltravers was wearing a green short-sleeved sport shirt and yellow slacks. For some reason, I was fascinated by the hair on his arms. There was so much of it! Too bad it wasn't on his head.

He listened quietly, leaning back and rocking slightly in his chair, while we gave him a laundered account of the moaning sounds we'd heard in the house: how we'd thought it was just the wind at first, but how we were sure, now, that it was something else.

"Something else?" he repeated. "Like what? Don't tell me you kids think Stoneycraig is haunted!"

His manner was politely skeptical and his face unreadable. I wondered what he was really thinking.

"Well . . . yes," I admitted. "We do."

"By whom? Or by what?"

Peter and I exchanged furtive glances. We'd agreed in advance not to say who we thought the ghost was. We figured it might be better to let Mr. Maltravers tell us, if he knew.

"By whom?" Mr. Maltravers repeated in a slightly louder voice, as if we were hard of hearing.

"We aren't sure," Peter told him reluctantly, "but we think it's a woman. It sounds like a woman, anyway."

"A sobbing woman," I put in. "Her crying is absolutely heartbreaking."

"A sobbing woman? You think Stoneycraig is haunted by the ghost of a sobbing woman?" He sounded disbelieving, but I noticed that he'd suddenly gone gray around his mouth and nose and that his nostrils looked pinched.

"You didn't say anything to Matt Hadley about a ghost last night," he said quietly, bringing his chair upright. "He says you told him it was the wind that frightened Clare."

Peter and I looked at each other again, this time in amazement. Neither of us had expected the news about last night to get out this fast.

Mr. Maltravers seemed to read our minds. "I just came from Matt's house," he explained. "He called me this morning and said he's ready to sell Stoneycraig."

"And . . . and you actually want to *buy* it?" Peter asked.

Mr. Maltravers nodded. "Yes. It's a piece of local history. I'd like to own it."

"Even after what we just told you about the ghost?"

Mr. Maltravers shrugged. "I don't mean to put you kids down, but I'm not superstitious. I'm a Realtor, remember? I can't afford to believe ghost stories about any of the houses I represent."

I noticed, though, that his face still had that gray, pinched look to it. As a matter of fact, he looked even worse now than before. I wondered if he was worrying about what the story of a ghost would do to the value of his property.

"Look, Mr. Maltravers," I said. "Before you decide to buy that house—there's something else we haven't told you. It might make you change your mind."

I looked over at Peter, who nodded, indicating

that I should take over this part of the story. I cleared my throat and tried to figure out the best way to begin.

Mr. Maltravers sat perfectly still. Waiting.

"Yes," I repeated, nodding. "There *is* something else you should know about Stoneycraig. I know it sounds crazy, but we're sure there's a second ghost."

Again, he didn't say anything, but, looking into his ice blue eyes, I could see his pupils contract like a cat's.

"He . . . it . . . plays the piano," I said.

"The piano?" Mr. Maltravers asked slowly. "Stoneycraig has a ghost who plays the piano?"

"What I mean is, he plays this one song all the time on the piano," I replied lamely.

"A song? What song?"

"Maybe you aren't familiar with it. It's from the eighties and it's been real popular for a long time and . . . "

I realized I was babbling. Would Mr. Maltravers take me seriously?

"What's the name of the song?" he asked again, staring intently at me.

Peter came to my rescue. "It's called 'Until Forever.' Do you know it?"

Mr. Maltravers took so long in answering that I began to think he'd never heard of it. His answer, when it came, surprised me.

"Yes, of course," he said. "Doesn't everybody know 'Until Forever'?"

I hurried on. "And that's not all. We found the sheet music tucked in the piano, under the lid. It was handwritten and signed by Stephen D'Amato. That's the weird part."

"Sheet music? Handwritten sheet music? And signed by Stephen D'Amato?"

The gray around his nose and mouth had spread to his whole face now. Or at least it seemed to. The light was poor in his office, though. The fluorescent light directly above his desk must have needed to be replaced, because it kept flickering and flickering. I figured that was what was giving him that odd color and wondered if I looked that bad, too.

Peter spoke up. "What we want to know, Mr. Maltravers, is—do you know whether or not Stephen really wrote that song?"

Mr. Maltravers shook his head in bewilderment. "Forgive me if I seem puzzled, but you're laying some pretty strong stuff on me here. A sobbing woman. A ghost who plays the piano . . . "

"I know it sounds unbelievable," I said, "but—"

"No, Stephen didn't write that song," Mr. Maltravers interrupted in a loud, firm voice. "Not to my knowledge. Stephen never had that much talent."

I sat back, relieved. "I didn't see how he could have. Everybody in Pedlar's Green would have known about it if he had, wouldn't they?"

Mr. Maltravers threw out his hands in a helpless gesture. "I would certainly think so. Especially me, as close as I am to the Hadleys."

"We don't know what to do," I told him. "We're just about at the breaking point. That weeping. The piano playing."

"You poor kids," Mr. Maltravers said sympathetically. "You must have been scared half out of your wits. There has to be a rational explanation for this, though. Why didn't you tell me about it the first time it happened?"

"I don't know," I confessed. "It sounded so crazy. I guess we were afraid you wouldn't believe us."

"Like I said," Mr. Maltravers said earnestly, "all the old houses around here have spooky stories connected with them. I've certainly never heard about that sobbing woman at Stoneycraig, though, or the phantom piano player."

He leaned back in his chair again. "Let's run through this thing one more time. You say you found a piece of sheet music. The music to 'Until Forever'?"

"That's right," Peter replied.

"Did you bring it?" he asked. "I'd sure like to see it."

"No," I said. "We left it at home. It was old and fragile and—"

"I hope you left it in a safe place."

"Yes," I said. "We put it in a drawer in the kitchen."

"Have you told anyone else about it?" Mr. Maltravers asked.

"No," Peter said. "We haven't even told Clare or Mr. Hadley. Right now, Marnie and I figure the important thing is to do something about that sobbing and piano playing every night. We're about to go around the bend."

"Yes," I put in. "Do you think we should call in someone to exorcize—if that's the right word—the music room?"

Mr. Maltravers reached across the desk and

patted my hand. "Just take it easy now, okay? Go home. Relax. Don't talk to anyone about this until I can figure out what's happening."

He glanced down at his watch. "Why don't I come over in a couple of hours and we'll discuss this further? I was thinking about coming anyway. I don't think you two should be alone in the house when the big storm hits."

"What big storm?" Peter asked. "We haven't listened to a radio or read a newspaper in two days."

"There's one headed our way. I just heard the weather bulletin. I thought I'd better come over and sit it out with you kids. We get some bad storms here on the coast. They can be scary when you aren't used to them."

Peter and I stood up. "We ought to get going, then," I said, tucking my shoulder bag under my arm. "I wouldn't want to be out on that little road that leads to Stoneycraig when it hits. It's got some pretty sharp curves."

"Thanks, Mr. Maltravers," Peter said. "We really appreciate everything you're doing for us."

"Yes," I put in. "I feel better already."

"Heck, it's nothing," replied Mr. Maltravers with a broad smile. "You kids just go on home and wait for me. I have a couple of things to do, but I'll get there before the storm, don't worry."

He rose from his chair and escorted us to the door. "I'm sure we can sort this ghost thing out. In the meantime, like I told you, let's just keep it between the three of us."

Later, in the car, I said to Peter, "He said he's

really close to the Hadleys. That's not what Mrs. Gleason says."

Peter switched on the ignition. "And that's not the only thing he said that's not accurate."

"What else?"

Peter grinned and gunned the motor. "He made a grammatical error. It's not *between* the three of us. He should have said *among* the three of us."

18

It was only midafternoon when Mr. Maltravers arrived at Stoneycraig, but already it was beginning to grow dark.

I was nervous. They say a cat's fur stands up just before a storm, and that's exactly how I was feeling now.

I've always hated storms. The first one here had been bad enough, but this time I knew what would happen to the electricity at Stoneycraig, and I dreaded it. I'd begun to associate darkness with *Her*—the sobbing woman. I was sure I couldn't take another night of her crying, while that creepy old piano played "Until Forever" over and over again.

Well, at least this time those two notes wouldn't keep coming up missing!

It was comforting to see Mr. Maltravers come through the front door. His bulk was reassuring. Even the roll of stomach that hung over his belt

made me feel safer somehow. There certainly
wasn't anything ghostly-looking about *that!*

"Whoo-ee!" he said, hanging on to the door to
keep the wind from tearing it from his fingers. "I
guess I made it just in time! I had to turn my lights
on to see the road."

"Listen to the thunder," Peter said, shutting the
door behind Mr. Maltravers. "It's moving in
closer."

I shivered and patted the back of my jeans,
checking to see if my mini Maglite was still in my
pocket. I'd stuck it there the minute it started
growing dark. I wasn't about to get caught
tonight stumbling around the house without a
flashlight.

Mr. Maltravers was carrying a leather attaché
case. He waggled it at us cheerfully. "A Realtor's
work is never done!"

He slipped off his raincoat and draped it over
the banister. "This storm is supposed to last for at
least a couple of hours. Hey, I sure could go for a
hot cup of coffee."

No sooner had we gone into the kitchen when
the storm hit.

The room suddenly darkened. I snapped on the
lights, but the next bolt of lightning knocked out
the electricity, just as I'd feared.

Peter and I hurriedly lit the hurricane lamps we'd
filled earlier and set out on the table in readiness.

More flashes of lightning zigzagged across the
sky, coming closer and closer as the thunder rum-
bled and rolled.

Then came the howling and shrieking of the

wind. It was blowing at what must have been gale force as it swept toward us from the sea, driving solid sheets of rain before it.

The rain came at the house horizontally, lashing it savagely, furiously. The foundations of the house almost seemed to shake and rumble in response.

I looked around uneasily. "It sounds like we could be blown out to sea."

Mr. Maltravers only laughed and sat down at the table. "Stoneycraig's weathered a lot of these storms. Don't worry about her. She'll still be here tomorrow."

I got out the instant coffee for Mr. Maltravers and some tea bags for Peter and me. Then I filled the teakettle and lit the gas burner under it. In no time at all, it was whistling cheerfully.

As I was setting the hot, steaming mugs on the table, a bolt of lightning lit up every corner of the kitchen, followed instantly by an ear-shattering thunderclap that sounded almost as if it were in the room with us.

Peter and I stared at each other with wide, frightened eyes. I was trembling from head to foot.

Mr. Maltravers gave a low whistle. "That one was close. Really close." He shook his head. "We're lucky it didn't hit the house."

Peter made his way unsteadily over to the phone and put the receiver to his ear. "I figured this would happen," he said. "No dial tone. Nothing. That bolt of lightning must have knocked out our line."

"Well, that's one way to get away from annoying phone calls," Mr. Maltravers said.

His feeble attempt at humor seemed to irritate Peter. "Maybe you don't realize this, Mr. Maltravers," he said coldly, "but Marnie and I are totally cut off from the rest of the world without a phone."

"And it will probably take days for them to repair the lines, too," I added. I'd stopped trembling and started worrying about what Dad would think if he called and couldn't get through.

"No it won't," Mr. Maltravers said. "I'll contact the phone company just as soon as I get back to the office. You'll have phone service again before you know it. You kids are real worrywarts."

He picked up his coffee and took a couple of deep swallows.

"Okay," he said, laying down the cup and wiping his mouth with the back of his hand. "I've come here to talk about that ghost thing, so let's talk. You kids haven't told anybody else about the sheet music, have you?"

"No, of course not," Peter replied. He came back to the table and sat down, dabbling his tea bag up and down in the hot water. "You told us not to say anything, remember?"

Mr. Maltravers nodded approvingly. "Good. I'd like to take a look at it, if you don't mind."

"I put it in here for safekeeping," I told him, opening a kitchen drawer and gently removing the yellowed pages.

I smoothed the paper flat when I laid it before Mr. Maltravers. Then I sat down beside him. "See?" I said, pointing. "There's his name right there, and look at what he's written beneath it. He's dedicated the song to Ellen and their baby."

Mr. Maltravers bent over the paper, frowning.

"Well, what do you think?" I prompted.

He didn't reply for a moment. Then he muttered, "Yeah, that's it, all right."

"You mean you've seen it before?" Peter asked.

Mr. Maltravers looked up. He had a strange, guarded expression on his face. "No. I only meant that it's definitely Stephen D'Amato's handwriting." His voice was flat and full of hatred.

"Are you sure?" Peter asked, leaning across the table for a closer look.

"Yes, I'm sure," Mr. Maltravers said from between clenched teeth.

I shook my head in bewilderment. "I don't understand. Does this mean he actually wrote the song?"

Mr. Maltravers reached down and picked up the attaché case at his feet. Then he set it on the table and unsnapped the fasteners.

I noticed with surprise that he'd turned pale—that gray, pinched pallor again. A muscle twitched and jerked in his jaw. But it was his eyes that scared me. They were wild. Crazy-looking.

He snatched up the sheet music, rolling it carelessly and jamming it into the top pocket of the case.

"Mr. Maltravers," I gasped. "What are you—?"

"Be quiet!" he barked, pulling something from his case and pointing it at me. It looked like a small black cylinder. Then I heard a hissing sound, a *psssst*, and suddenly my eyes felt as if they were on fire.

The pain was unbearable. I leaped to my feet, clapping my hands to my face. Hot tears streamed through my fingers.

"Help me, Peter!" I screamed. "I'm blind!"

19

As I stood there, half-crazy with fear and pain, my hands covering my streaming eyes, I was dimly aware of another hissing of the cylinder and Peter's strangled cry. Then the sounds of a struggle. A chair overturning. A cup crashing to the floor.

Rough hands did something to my ankles, binding them together, and I was pushed back down in my chair. My hands were yanked from my face and tied behind my back.

"Please—" I sobbed. "My eyes! My eyes!"

The sound of running water. The welcome feeling of a cold, wet cloth on my eyes.

"Peter!" I moaned.

"I'm here, Marnie." His voice came in short gasps. "He . . . he got me, too!"

"I'm blind!" I cried.

"No you're not, you stupid little whiner," Mr. Maltravers replied impatiently. "It's only pepper spray. You'll get over the effects in a few minutes."

More thunder rumbling and rolling outside. Not as loud now, but still close. The wind and rain hadn't lessened, though.

The terrible stinging was beginning to subside.

"Are you okay, Peter?" I managed to call out.

"Yeah." There was relief in his voice. "I'm . . . I'm all right now."

"I can't believe you city kids aren't familiar with pepper spray," jeered Mr. Maltravers. "Or that you'd be such babies about it."

I yanked helplessly at my cords. Not only was I bound hand and foot, but he'd also tied me to the chair. "What are you doing to us, Mr. Maltravers? Let us go. Please."

"Not now. Just sit there and shut up."

After what seemed an eternity, the cloth was removed and I cautiously opened my eyes. They were still sore and runny, but I could see.

Mr. Maltravers went around the table and removed the wet towel from Peter's eyes, too.

Peter struggled to sit erect. He looked around, blinking rapidly, tears still streaming from his inflamed eyes. "What's going on?" he asked dazedly, pulling against his ropes. "Why'd you do that, Mr. Maltravers?"

"Because I wanted to tie you both up without having to knock you out first. I want you awake and aware of what's happening, and why I'm doing what I'm doing. It's part of your punishment."

"P-punishment? For what?" I stammered.

"For trying to uncover the past. Curiosity always kills the cat, you know."

Peter and I stared at each other in red-eyed terror. He looked as frightened as I did.

The man was crazy. Flat-out crazy. What was he going to do to us?

Mr. Maltravers sat down at the head of the table.

"You can't get away with this," I said wildly. "We're . . . we're expecting company."

Mr. Maltravers only laughed. "Nice try, but nobody's out visiting in this weather."

"There's been a terrible mistake," I said, giving my ropes another futile tug. "I still don't know what you think we've done."

"You don't? Then I'll tell you," he said. "It was a real shock when you kids came in this morning and told me you'd found that sheet music. I nearly blew it."

"What do you know about that sheet music?" I demanded, remembering now how pale he'd turned when I first mentioned it.

"Everything. For starters, I was the one who stuck it down in the piano sixteen years ago. I meant to go back and get it, but I forgot."

He shook his head in amazement. "Funny, isn't it, that I could forget something that important? I must have blanked it out after I—"

"Let us go, Mr. Maltravers," Peter broke in. "We don't know anything about that music. I promise we won't tell a soul about it if you'll only let us go."

Mr. Maltravers settled back in his chair and gave Peter a sly smile.

"Gimme a break, kid. Do you really think I'm

that dumb? No, I can't let you go now. It's too late."

"No, no it isn't!" I cried. "We'll just—"

"Forget it," Mr. Maltravers barked. "Letting you go is not an option. You know too much now. That handwritten sheet music proves that Stephen D'Amato wrote 'Until Forever,' and that I had a motive for killing him." He laughed wildly. "I had *lots* of motives for murdering Stephen D'Amato!"

"You *murdered* Stephen D'Amato?" I asked shrilly. "He was *murdered?* But everybody says he ran away."

"No, he didn't. He's here, right here, under this house."

Another zigzag of lightning. Another clap of thunder.

My mouth felt like cotton, and my heart was beating so hard I was afraid it would burst right out of my body. Peter was trembling visibly.

"His dead b-body is under this house?" Peter quavered.

Mr. Maltravers nodded. "You see, I've always believed that the punishment should fit the crime. Stephen D'Amato's crime was to marry the girl I loved, so his punishment is to stay here in her house for all eternity."

He glared first at Peter and then me. "Ellen was mine. But she went off to New York City and came home married—and, as we all found out later, pregnant. I pretended to be a good sport about the marriage, but inside I wanted to hurt Stephen. Hurt him bad. Make him suffer."

He paused, breathing heavily, before continuing.

"Matt Hadley wasn't happy about the marriage either. He figured anybody who did nothing but write songs all day was either lazy or stupid. But he had to accept it. After all, Ellen was his only child.

"He wanted to do the right thing by Ellen, though, so he took out a second mortgage on Stoneycraig and used the money to fix the house up for a wedding present. When I inspected the house for the bank loan, I accidentally found the hiding place."

"Hiding place?" Peter broke in. "What hiding place?"

"The one they used for the Underground Railroad," Mr. Maltravers said, getting up from his chair. "The Hadley family must have closed it up and forgotten about it after the Civil War."

He went over to the fireplace and slipped behind the stove. Then he stuck his hand up the chimney and pressed something.

The back of the fireplace swung inward. What had been solid stone was now a gaping hole. A foul, musty odor seeped into the room.

I shrank back in horror.

Mr. Maltravers came out from behind the stove and stood before the fireplace, his hands clasped behind his back, rocking back and forth on his heels.

"I knew, right from the start, that I would have to kill Stephen," he said, "but I wasn't sure how or when I would do it. And then they announced Ellen's pregnancy. That's when I knew the time had come to kill Stephen."

He looked to us for sympathy but got none. I

could only stare past him at that dark, evil-smelling hole. Why was he showing it to us?

"I waited until the baby was almost due," he went on. "Stephen would seem like a monster if he deserted his wife just before the baby came. That was a touch of genius, don't you think?"

He shrugged unconcernedly when neither of us replied.

"Finally Ellen went off to the hospital. She'd gone into false labor, but they decided to keep her there for observation. It was the perfect time. I made sure Stephen was alone in the house and then I let myself in. He was in the music room. I crept up the stairs as quietly as I could."

He frowned, remembering. "That was the first time I'd heard 'Until Forever.' I didn't know anything about music, but even I could tell that this one was going to be a winner. As I came down the hall, I got angrier and angrier. Stephen had Ellen and the baby that would soon be born. And now he had a song that would probably make him rich and famous. It just wasn't fair!"

Mr. Maltravers's face hardened.

"I'd already decided what I'd use for a murder weapon," he went on. "The silver candelabra. It was heavy enough, and it was always there, on the piano.

"Stephen was playing his song, lost in thought. I sneaked up behind him, reached out and picked up the candelabra. Stephen spun around, surprised, but I was faster. I smashed the heavy end of the candelabra down on his head. It killed him right away."

He seemed to enjoy this part. I wondered, with a shudder, how often he thought about it.

I squeezed my eyes as tightly shut as I could. "Please . . . please, Mr. Maltravers!" I cried. "Don't tell us any more. It's too awful!"

"Then I heard this babbling," Mr. Maltravers went on, as if he hadn't heard me. "Little Orvie Gleason was standing in the doorway. That fool was always hanging around Stoneycraig. I wondered if I was going to have to kill him, too. It would have been a hard job. Orvie's big and powerful. But he ran away before I could decide what to do. I realized then that no one would believe him, even if he did manage to make himself understood. Besides, I had an alibi. I was supposed to be out of town that day. My secretary would swear to that."

He gestured to the opening in the fireplace. "After Orvie left, I dragged Stephen down the stairs and opened the secret door."

Peter swallowed hard. "And so that . . . that's where he's buried?"

"No, not buried. I wouldn't do that much for him. I just threw him down there, like the piece of garbage he is," Mr. Maltravers said with evident satisfaction.

And then he added, "But you'll see that for yourself when you join him."

2O

Buried alive!

Mr. Maltravers was going to bury us alive in that stinking hole alongside the bones of Stephen D'Amato!

Peter lunged and yanked at his ropes, but they wouldn't give. He even tried to scoot his chair over to Mr. Maltravers, as if, in his growing desperation, he hoped to do some damage to the madman with his feet.

Mr. Maltravers picked up the can of pepper spray and aimed it at Peter. "I can do this again, you know, if you don't settle down. Believe me, it's no use to struggle."

He was right. It *was* useless. Peter slumped back in his chair, his head down.

If only we could keep Mr. Maltravers talking, I thought, maybe he'd say something revealing, something we could use to change his mind.

When your back is up against the wall, you'll try anything.

"Wait a minute!" I cried. "You can't possibly get away with this!"

"Why not?" demanded Mr. Maltravers.

"Because Peter and I can't just disappear. There'll be an all-out search for us."

Mr. Maltravers laughed. "A lot of people disappear in storms. You were last seen visiting my office. I'll say you talked about going down to your beach to watch the storm come in. I, of course, urged you not to do it, told you it was too dangerous, but evidently you didn't listen."

He heaved a mock sigh. "How sad. Another pair of stupid kids drowned because they took foolish risks."

I tried again. "Mrs. Gleason's coming in Monday morning. She'll hear us down there."

"No she won't. That place was designed to hide runaway slaves, remember? It's built deep under the house, almost like a bomb shelter. Rest assured, the first Mr. Hadley built it solid and soundproof."

Peter had raised his head and was watching Mr. Maltravers. I could almost see the wheels turning in his head. The two of us were usually on the same wavelength. I hoped we were now.

I closed my eyes and sent him the silent message, *Keep him talking. Keep him talking.*

"If you're going to kill us, Mr. Maltravers, you can at least tell us what we're dying for," Peter said.

"What?" Mr. Maltravers said, surprised.

"You know. The sheet music," replied Peter. "You're killing us because we found the sheet music. I still don't understand."

"It's very simple," Mr. Maltravers told him. "After I killed Stephen, I went to New York and sold the song. Under a fictitious name, of course."

He shrugged. "Now I have a Swiss bank account that's getting fatter every day, thanks to 'Until Forever.' That's why I didn't want you telling anyone about finding that other copy—the one in the piano. If it ever came out that someone else is getting royalties for a song Stephen wrote, I could be in real trouble. Besides, it might reopen the investigation into his disappearance."

"But what was that sheet music doing stuck down in the strings of the piano?" Peter asked.

"Wait a minute—" I broke in. "The ghost music. It must be the ghost of Stephen D'Amato, then, that keeps playing 'Until Forever' on that piano."

"Impossible," snapped Mr. Maltravers. "You're making up that ghost music stuff just to frighten me. You found the sheet music and decided to pretend that Stephen's ghost has been playing it."

"No, we haven't. And what about the sobbing woman?" I asked. "Admit it, Mr. Maltravers. When I told you about her, you looked scared to death."

"I did not!" he shouted. "I don't believe in ghosts. There aren't any ghosts in Stoneycraig!"

"Then why does everybody in Pedlar's Green act like they think it's haunted?" I asked.

"I planted those stories," Mr. Maltravers said. "After Ellen's death, I decided to buy the house. I wanted to live where she'd lived—and I wanted to keep my secret about Stephen safe. So I figured that if I made the house sound bad enough, no one else would want it. It worked. Matt Hadley has finally decided to sell, and I'm the only buyer."

"About that sheet music, though——" Peter said.

"But Stoneycraig *is* haunted, Mr. Maltravers," I insisted. "*She*—the ghost—has got to be Ellen, and you're responsible. It's your fault she committed suicide. She was so unhappy about Stephen's disappearance that . . . "

I stopped talking when I saw his face. He really looked crazy now. It was his eyes. I felt like I was gazing into the merciless, inhuman eyes of a shark.

"Ellen didn't commit suicide," he said slowly. "I killed her."

"*You killed Ellen Hadley?*" Peter cried.

"Yes. And I put the sheet music in the piano when . . . Well, I was confused. It's not every day you kill the woman you love."

Another flash of lightning lit up the sky. For one brief moment, I thought I saw a face at the window. Orvie? But then I blinked and the face disappeared.

Am I hallucinating? I thought wildly.

"But why did you kill her?" Peter demanded. "You said you loved her!"

"I didn't want to kill her. She made me," Mr. Maltravers said self-righteously. "It was all her fault. I was even going to marry her. Eventually."

"What do you mean, she *made* you kill her?" I demanded.

"She found the signed copy of the song, the one dedicated to her." He gestured toward his attaché case. "That one. The song had become an instant hit. Ellen heard it on the radio and recognized it."

"But—" I said.

"Evidently Stephen had planned to give the sheet music to her as a homecoming gift," Mr. Maltravers continued. "She was pretty excited when she found it and asked me to come over. She said it proved he hadn't deserted her after all, that he wouldn't have written that dedication if he'd been planning to split."

He paused. "That's why I had to kill her. She was talking about taking it to the police. So I killed her with the candelabra, just as I had Stephen. Then I carried her down to the cliff and threw her over."

The candelabra! It was always on the floor after a haunting!

"I did make one mistake, though, didn't I?" asked Mr. Maltravers. "Before I carried her body down to the cliff, I tucked the sheet music under the piano lid, intending to come back later. But, like I said, I forgot."

"You're not going to get away with this, you know," Peter said threateningly.

"Yes, I will. And now, if what you say is true, there'll be four ghosts in the house instead of two." He snickered. "At least you'll have company."

He looked up at the kitchen clock. "My, my, how time flies when you're having a good time," he said coldly. "I'd better finish what I started."

Going over to the cutting board, he took a long, sharp butcher knife from the wall holder.

"No!" I screamed. "Don't! Please!"

Mr. Maltravers came up behind Peter and raised the knife.

"No!" I screamed again.

With two quick slashes, Mr. Maltravers severed the rope that bound Peter to the chair and dragged him over to the fireplace.

Peter bucked and struggled, but Mr. Maltravers held him fast under one arm, holding the knife to his throat with the other.

I hadn't realized how strong Mr. Maltravers was. There were muscles under that flab after all. He hauled Peter, still wriggling and resisting, to the opening in the wall and shoved him in.

Mr. Maltravers turned to me. "It's a long way down. There used to be a flight of stairs there, but they're gone. I do hope your cousin didn't break his neck when he landed."

"Peter!" I shrieked. "Peter!"

No reply.

The last thing I saw before I fainted was Mr. Maltravers coming toward me, smiling.

21

I awoke in pitch blackness on a cold dirt floor. Every bone in my body ached. At first I couldn't remember where I was. Then it came to me.

I was buried alive in Stephen D'Amato's tomb!

"Oh, God," I sobbed. "Somebody please help me."

"Marnie?" said a weak voice. "Are you okay?"

"Peter!" I cried. "I thought you were dead!"

"It was a long drop, but I'm not dead. I don't think anything's broken, either. How about you?"

I made a few cautious tests. "I'm all right," I said. "Everything hurts, but I can move my arms and legs. Oh, Peter . . . what are we going to do?"

"Listen, Marnie, can you hear anything?"

It was silent. So silent. I couldn't even hear the howling of the wind or the sound of the thunder.

"No, I can't hear a thing," I told him despairingly. "Mr. Maltravers was right. We're underneath the house. We can't hear anything, and no one can hear us."

"I hoped he was lying," Peter said in a hollow monotone. "I hoped that maybe, if we shouted and screamed, Mrs. Gleason would hear us when she came in Monday morning."

"It's so dark in here," I said, shuddering. "If only we could see."

"This place was used by the Underground Railroad, remember?" Peter said. "Maybe it's more than just a secret room. Maybe it leads somewhere."

"I doubt that," I said. "Mr. Maltravers would know about it if it did, wouldn't he?"

"Well, what's the use of wondering? We can't go anywhere if we can't see," Peter said hopelessly. "I don't have any matches or a lighter on me. Nothing. Not that I could even get to them," he added.

I moved my bound hands over to my back jeans pocket. Yes, my mini flashlight was still there. I could feel it.

"Wait a minute," I said. "I've got my Maglite in my pocket. If we could just untie these ropes, we'd be able to look around."

Peter didn't say anything for a couple of minutes. I could hear him breathing heavily in the darkness. Finally he said, "Marnie, do you remember that movie where those two undercover agents sat back-to-back and untied each other? Do you think we could do that?"

"What have we got to lose?" I replied.

I heard him grunt and puff as he rolled toward me. I dragged myself up to a sitting position.

"Let me do yours," I directed, groping around

behind me for his hands. "We've got to lean back against each other to keep our balance. It might take a long time to do this."

I managed to untie Peter's ropes. It was easier than I'd expected. Mr. Maltravers had done a good job of wrapping the rope tightly around Peter's wrists, but he'd finished it up with what felt like a couple of simple square knots, and I was able to pick them loose.

"The Maglite's in my left pocket," I directed. "Reach in and get it. If you turn it on and set it on the ground, we'll both be able to see."

In the thin beam of the flashlight, Peter untied the ropes around his ankles and then freed me. We helped each other up, moaning a little at the prickles of pain that shot up our legs.

I adjusted the light and shone it upward at the wall behind the fireplace. "Maybe that hidden door opens from the inside, too," I suggested hopefully. "If we could just climb up high enough, maybe we could push it open."

"It's too high," Peter replied. "Even if you stood on my shoulders, it would still be too high. Mr. Maltravers said there used to be some wooden steps that led down. Give me that flashlight, Marnie."

He took the light from me and started flashing it around. "No, what's left has rotted and fallen all apart. I was hoping that maybe we could—"

His voice broke off abruptly.

"What is it?" I said.

"Stephen D'Amato," Peter said in a hoarse whisper.

I looked in the direction of the beam. Ahead, something white gleamed in the shadows.

Bones. What was left of Stephen D'Amato was lying there.

Stephen D'Amato. Ellen's husband. Clare's father.

Stephen D'Amato, who'd written that beautiful love song, and who really had loved his wife and unborn child, in spite of what everyone thought.

Beside me, Peter drew in a quivering breath.

"Look at him, Peter," I said, my voice trembling. "It's so unfair. He was murdered. But everyone thought he ran away. That he deserted his wife and baby. And now even his own daughter thinks he was a terrible person. But the worst part of it, the very worst part, is that his body was treated like a piece of garbage. That's what Mr. Maltravers said, remember? He said he threw him down in here like a piece of garbage."

I remembered the music room. The cold. The feeling of hopelessness and despair. No wonder. And I thought of Ellen, weeping for herself and her murdered husband—

Her murdered husband who was now only a moldering heap of bones in the wavering beam of a flashlight.

"Stephen!" I yelled. "You're here. I know you're here. You and Ellen want us to help you, don't you? That's what all that haunting's been about, isn't it? We've done our best, but there's nothing we can do now unless you help us, too."

"Marnie?" Peter asked gently. "Are you okay?"

Suddenly I smelled it. The faint scent of Glenheather aftershave.

"Stephen?" I asked. "Is that you?"

"Stop it, Marnie," Peter commanded. "You're starting to act weird again."

"Can't you smell it?" I demanded.

Peter sniffed. "Smell what?"

I sniffed again, too. Nothing. The scent was gone now.

Had I imagined the Glenheather aftershave, or had the spirit of Stephen D'Amato been trying to send me a message?

But what kind of message—one meant to raise my hopes?

Or was he only trying to warn me of a coming danger?

22

Peter, of course, acted like he thought I'd gone off my nut.

Maybe I had. But on the other hand, maybe I hadn't. Maybe Stephen's spirit *had* been there, after all, called forth from that shadowy, unhappy place that still bound him to the earth.

If that was so, then Peter and I had a responsibility to do what we could, for as long as we could.

A clump of irregular rocks stood at the far end of the area. I went over to it and flashed the light around.

"You were right, Peter. This *is* more than just a hiding place. There's a tunnel beyond these rocks. It has to go *somewhere!*"

"So why didn't Mr. Maltravers know about it, then?" Peter asked worriedly. "Maybe it's dangerous, Marnie. There might be a drop-off or something."

"Mr. Maltravers didn't know about it because he

didn't come down here," I said. "From where he stood when he threw down Stephen's body, this place only looked like a secret room beneath the house."

We made our way around the rocks and shone the light down the tunnel.

"Yes, it *is* a tunnel, and a long one, too, from what I can see," Peter exclaimed. "I wonder where it goes."

"Listen, Peter," I said, thinking hard. "Do you remember when we were down there on the beach, and we wondered if the fugitive slaves were brought to our cove and ferried out when the tide was low?"

"Yes," Peter said, "and I know what you're getting at—that maybe this tunnel leads to the cove, right?"

"Right. But we didn't see any holes in the side of the cliff that day."

"If this tunnel leads down to the cove, there must be an opening somewhere," Peter said thoughtfully. "Or at least there *was* one, back in those days. Maybe it's covered up now, though."

"It might have been closed by a mud slide," I put in grimly. "Or the sea could have washed up boulders against it. In that case, we're trapped."

"We can't think like that, Marnie," Peter said. "We've got to go for it. We might have to dig our way out with our bare hands, but what other choice do we have?"

I led the way, carrying the flashlight.

The tunnel was narrow, so narrow that I had to

keep my elbows pressed up closely against my sides.

I remembered all the adventure movies I'd seen where the heroine's flashlight gives out at the crucial moment, and I tried to remember the last time I'd put new AAA batteries in mine.

I couldn't, but my little metal Maglite seemed to be giving out a good strong beam for its size.

"The ceiling's getting lower," Peter said. "Be careful. Don't hit your head."

"The floor's dropping, too," I answered. "We must be going downhill."

Not only that, but the tunnel was curving. We were soon going around a series of sharp bends. I had to stop and take a couple of deep breaths to steady my nerves. I've been a little claustrophobic ever since I was stuck in an elevator a couple of years ago. It wasn't for long, but I will never forget the panic I felt at being trapped and enclosed as I hung in that tiny little cage between floors.

Peter knew how I felt about being confined in small spaces, and I could hear the anxiety in his voice when he asked, "Are you okay, Marnie?"

"Yeah," I muttered. "Sort of."

"The builders must have hit some pretty solid rock right about here," Peter observed, talking in this matter-of-fact voice, scrunching down even lower as the ceiling dropped still further. I knew he was trying to distract me, to make me focus on something other than my claustrophobia. "They had to tunnel around it, I guess."

As the tunnel grew smaller and more restricting, I concentrated on my breathing, keeping it slow and even. I'd begun to hyperventilate a little, and my heart was beating too quickly. I had to stop this thing before it went out of control.

The ceiling dropped lower. We had to walk doubled over at the waist. Then at a semicrouch.

"The walls are getting rockier. They must have had a hard time digging through them," Peter said in a strained voice.

"Yes," I agreed, trying to sound normal. "The builders didn't leave us much space, did they?"

Just thinking about those enclosing walls made me bite my lip in panic. There was no going back now because there was no way to turn around. Oh, God! Would I survive this thing?

I needed air. More air! Sweat broke out on my upper lip, and I heard a funny ringing in my ears. No! I mustn't give in to it. I mustn't let myself go. If I fainted, what would Peter do?

I had to keep moving.

Finally I said, my voice edged with panic. "We're going to have to go the rest of the way on our hands and knees, Peter. There's no other way."

But we needed light to do that. How could I hold the flashlight and crawl at the same time? Then I remembered the pictures I'd seen of coal miners and the way they always wore lights in their caps. My headband! I jammed the Maglite under my headband, arranging it so that it was pointed straight ahead, and started out again on all fours.

It was slow and painful going. Even though I was wearing jeans, the sharp, pointed rocks and pebbles bit through the cloth and hurt my knees. I tried to concentrate on the pain so I wouldn't think of the way the walls were closing in on me.

It was no use. I crawled forward, my arms trembling with weariness. It seemed as if we'd been on our knees for hours. I was breathing too fast and not drawing in enough air. It was dank and close down there, and it smelled of desperation. Maybe those long-ago fugitive slaves had imprinted their emotions, like fingerprints, on the walls of the tunnel.

How did they do it, those fugitives? Especially after all the hardships they'd already endured just getting here. And what about the children? And the babies? Did the parents strap them to their bodies? Could I have made it through this tunnel with the extra weight of a child—or maybe even two—on my back?

My breath came in sharp gasps now. Air. Were we running out of air? The ringing in my ears grew louder as I thought about what it would be like to suffocate. The drawing in of thick, wet . . . nothing. My chest heaved. I was covered with sweat.

Finally I lay down flat on the floor of the tunnel. "Can you crawl over me?" I asked weakly. "I'm not going to make it, Peter. You're going to have to go on without me."

"Don't talk dumb, Marnie. I'm not going on alone," he snapped. "Don't weird out on me now. You've never been a quitter before."

"I'm not a quitter!" I protested, raising my head.

"Then prove it!" Peter said. "Get up, Marnie. Prove you're not a quitter."

I hauled myself up to a crawling position again

and started out slowly—right arm out, left knee forward. Left arm out, right knee forward.

"Concentrate on your breathing," Peter commanded. "Deep breaths. In and out. In and out."

I did as he said, and felt better. Stronger. The ringing in my ears had stopped, too. I kept moving, more regularly now and a little faster.

"That's it," Peter encouraged. "That's my girl."

"*Your* girl?" I said with a wobbly laugh. "Now who's weirding out?"

"I'm not weirding out," Peter replied shortly. "You've always been my girl. Come on, Marnie. Move it. This tunnel has to lead somewhere. It can't go on forever."

I forced myself to move even faster, determined to show Peter I was no quitter.

It didn't seem quite as airless in here as it had before. I still felt confined by the narrowness of the tunnel, but my panic attack had passed.

"You okay now?" Peter asked.

"Yes, I think so," I said, barely avoiding a sharp rock in my path. Then, "What did you mean, Peter, about me always being your girl? What about those others—Debbi Sue Tipton and Bambi Levine and—"

"They were just a phase," Peter said. "I'm older now. And wiser."

"Oh yeah?"

"Yeah." Peter reached out and grabbed my ankle, pulling me to a halt. "Listen, Marnie, being away all those months made me do some serious thinking. Every evening at Ecclecleuch Manor I used to sit there in the library and look at that painting of the queen with the long, frizzy red hair—the one that reminded me of you, remember?"

"Frizzy red hair! *Frizzy?*"

"And I realized that I missed you more than anybody. I missed you very much." His voice rose. "In spite of the fact that you've been a nuisance and a pain in the neck for as long as I can remember, yes, I missed you! And then I realized that all those other girls didn't matter. They didn't matter at all."

"You missed me so much that you came up here and got a big crush on Clare Hadley," I said bitterly and started crawling forward again, not heeding the sharp little pebbles under my knees.

There was a brief silence. Then Peter yanked on my leg again, bringing me to another halt.

"Okay, Marnie," he said. "You probably won't understand this, what with your hot temper and all, but—"

"I do *not* have a hot temper. I don't know why you always blame everything on my hot temper."

Peter sighed. "Anyway, when I came home from Scotland, I was going to tell you how I felt."

"About my frizzy red hair?"

"Yeah. That, too," Peter said. "I like your hair. I've always liked it. But then, there you were—making a fool of yourself over that creepy Norman. You acted like you were in love with him or something."

"Me and Norman?" I asked, throwing grammar to the winds. "You've got to be kidding!"

"Well, you sure acted like you thought he was

Mr. Wonderful. Personally, I thought he was a worm."

"Actually, Peter," I confessed. "Norman *is* a worm."

"Now you tell me," he groaned. "So there was Clare. The princess in the tower. To tell you the truth, Marnie, part of it was that I felt sorry for her. She's had such an unhappy life. I mean, her father deserting her. And then her mother's suicide. The girl's a walking tragedy. And, yes, she is incredibly good-looking. What normal guy wouldn't find her interesting?"

"But did you really have to drool every time you looked at her?" I demanded.

"Marnie, if I hadn't been afraid you'd laugh at me, I wouldn't have even noticed Clare."

"You're kidding!"

"No. Cross my heart. I am *not* kidding," Peter swore.

For the first time in my life, I was totally speechless.

"Marnie? Say something, Marnie."

"You . . . you really like my hair?" I finally managed to say, as we crawled around yet another sharp bend.

Turning my head, I gazed soulfully, meaningfully, into his eyes. But Peter wasn't gazing back at me. He was squinting into the darkness. Then, with an abrupt gesture, he yanked the Maglite from my headband and shone it over my shoulder.

"We did it!" he yelled in a voice that made my eardrums pop. "Look! It's the end of the tunnel!"

I looked in the direction of the light. We were

now in what appeared to be an open space. It was only a few yards wide, but we could stand up again.

"Peter!" I cried. "I can't believe we made it!"

Peter took my arm and dragged me to my feet, shining the flashlight all around. Directly ahead of us was an uneven stone wall. The end of the line.

He moved closer, shining the light over and over again on the wall.

"We made it, all right," he said in a despairing voice, "but there's no opening. It doesn't look like there's ever been an opening in this wall."

I went over to the wall and felt around with my hands. Peter was right. There was no opening.

"Then it's hopeless," I said. "There's no way out. We're trapped in here, Peter. Trapped forever."

23

I was too tired and heartsick to cry.

To come so far, and to end like this.

"I guess this is it," I said. "We've had it." I sat down heavily on the ground, and leaned my back against one of the walls.

Peter dropped down beside me. "No, I refuse to believe it. There has to be an opening in that wall. The fugitives used this tunnel. So why would there be a tunnel if it didn't go anywhere?"

"There probably *was* an opening . . . once. . . ." I muttered. "But it's blocked off now. Face it, Peter. There's no way out."

"Better turn off the flashlight, Marnie," Peter advised. "We might need it later."

"For what?" I asked hopelessly. "Why don't we just lie down right now and die quietly. How long does it take to die, Peter, when you don't have any food or water? You used to be a Boy Scout. Tell me."

"Be quiet, Marnie," Peter snapped. "I'm trying to think."

I flashed the light around the floor of the enclosure one more time.

"Hey!" I exclaimed, pointing. "Look at that!"

The beam of light, directed into one of the corners, showed what appeared to be the remains of a small campfire, a campfire that must have burned a long, long time ago.

We scrambled to our feet and went over to it.

Charred pieces of firewood were stacked neatly over a blackened circle, as if the fire had been started and then hastily extinguished.

"See? I told you!" Peter cried. "The fugitive slaves really did use this tunnel! They must have kept a fire going while they waited to be picked up by the boat that took them to Canada!"

What had happened here? Had the waiting fugitives been suddenly called to the boat—and a new life? I hoped with all my heart that was it. I hoped the ending had been a happy one.

"I'm sure the entrance to the cave was here somewhere," Peter said, running his hands over the rocky surface. "We can find it, I know we can. Aim the light over here, Marnie."

I did and saw nothing. Nothing but an uneven rock wall.

"Where is it?" Peter asked desperately. "There's got to be some sign of the original entrance!"

"Wait a minute, Peter," I cried. "Maybe we're going at this thing all wrong."

I snapped the flashlight off.

"Hey! I can't see!" Peter protested.

"Back up. Back away from the wall," I commanded.

Both of us backed up and I waited for my eyes to become accustomed to the blackness. And then I saw it. A hair-thin crack of outside light outlining what had to be a narrow opening in the face of the rock.

"There it is!" I shrieked, my voice bounding off the walls. "There's the cave entrance!"

Half out of our heads with excitement, we scraped and jabbed at the wall with sharp stones and pieces of wood from the old campfire. The rocks and clay fell away quickly. Large, crumbling chunks dropped to our feet. We kicked them aside and kept on scraping.

"That storm probably helped us," Peter panted as he yanked a jumbo-sized stone from the wall. "This hole must have been plugged up for years with all the stuff that's fallen down from the cliff. The winds and rains coming in hard must have washed some of it away."

"Yes," I agreed. "The entrance was probably camouflaged by something in the beginning, and then all that other junk and debris just added to it. But how thick is it? Do you really think we can dig through it without proper tools?"

Using a thick stick as a spear, Peter jabbed at the portion of the wall behind the stone he'd just removed. It went through with very little resistance. Then he put his nose to the hole he'd made and sniffed cautiously. A grin split his face from ear to ear. "We sure can. Smell that, Marnie? Smell the ocean?"

Air. Fresh air. Air from the sea!

We dug and scraped like mad dogs. Peter had to punch out the last bit with his fist, and I stuck my head through. If I live to be a hundred, I'll never forget how I felt when I looked out and saw that beautiful, beautiful sky again.

Beautiful to me, anyway. It was gray and overcast. The wind was still blowing, but it had calmed down somewhat, and the rains had stopped.

"Just a little wider, Peter, and we can squeeze through," I said laughing from the pure joy of being alive.

Peter pulled me back into the cave, spun me around, and kissed me. Hard. I felt dizzy again, but this was definitely not a panic attack. This time, the dizziness felt pretty darn good.

I kissed him back. Finally he held me out at arm's length, his blue eyes smiling into mine. "We'll never get out of here if we don't get back to work."

The hole wasn't very big, but we managed to squeeze through. We had to crawl out backward and scramble down the side of the cliff, finding toeholds and clinging to roots. The beach had evidently dropped away from the cliff and moved farther out since this entrance had been used last.

Finally we were standing on the beach, up to our ankles in wet sand, with angry waves, the last of the storm, breaking on the rocks beyond and rushing up and washing against our legs.

We waded over to the stairs that would take us to the top of the cliff.

I stopped, one hand on the rail. "Wait a minute,

Peter," I said, "what if Mr. Maltravers is up there, waiting for us?"

"Why would he be?" Peter replied. "He thinks we're under the house, dying slowly. He's probably home by now. He won't want anybody to know he's been at Stoneycraig this afternoon."

The stairs seemed to go on forever. We climbed upward, pulling ourselves along by the rail. I hadn't realized how tired I was until now. All I wanted was a hot bath and the police, in that order.

"Wait a minute!" Peter held up his hand, waving me back, as we neared the top. "Maybe I'd better take a quick look around before we show ourselves. If Mr. Maltravers *is* still here, we'll have to hide on the beach and wait for him to go away."

I watched anxiously as he stuck his head up and looked toward the house.

Then he grinned. "Come on, Marnie!" he whooped, dragging me up the remaining steps. "We're home free!"

24

Three cars were parked in our driveway. One of them had a red light on its hood. The second was Mrs. Gleason's old Ford pickup. The third was a large blue Oldsmobile. It had to be Mr. Hadley's. I remembered seeing it parked in front of his house.

Mr. Maltravers's little Miata was nowhere in sight.

Peter grabbed my hand, and together we raced toward the house, shouting and waving our arms. With the wind blowing, they couldn't possibly have heard us, but we shouted, anyway.

Still shouting, we burst through the back door and into the kitchen.

And were greeted by a stunned silence.

I realized for the first time how we must look: red-eyed, wet, filthy, our hair sticking out wildly in all directions. Especially mine.

The local sheriff and his deputy were standing

by the stove, drinking coffee. They froze, coffee mugs in midair, as they stared at what must have looked like a couple of shrieking swamp monsters.

Clare was the first to recognize us. "Marnie! Peter!" she cried, throwing herself at us. "We didn't know what happened to you!"

I looked around the kitchen—at Mrs. Gleason, leaning against the sink shedding tears of joy; at Matt Hadley, who'd leaped to his feet from his chair at the table; at Little Orvie, calmly eating a toasted bagel; and finally at Clare, who was still hanging on to us. Well, to Peter, at least.

"What's everybody doing here?" I asked, puzzled. I turned to the sheriff. "How did you know Peter and I were in trouble?"

Mrs. Gleason answered for them. "Little Orvie saw you." She tore off a paper towel and blew her nose with gusto. "Thank heaven you're safe!"

"So it *was* you, Orvie, at the window!" I cried. "I'm so glad! I thought I was seeing things!"

Little Orvie smiled and went back to his bagel, his eyes as unreadable as ever.

"We received a call from Mr. Hadley," the sheriff told us. "Mrs. Gleason had contacted him."

"Yes," Mrs. Gleason went on. "Little Orvie started acting nervous and fidgety when the storm hit. I didn't know he'd gone up to Stoneycraig until he came home all excited and making those wild noises of his. I finally calmed him down. That's when I found out what he'd seen through the window—you two tied to chairs with Mr. Maltravers standing over you."

"Wait a minute, Mrs. Gleason," Peter interrupted, looking confused. "Little Orvie can't . . . well, you said he . . . "

Mrs. Gleason's eyes filled with tears again. She bit her lip, which had begun to tremble. "No, my Orvie still can't talk, but maybe I've learned to listen better."

She ripped off another paper towel and dabbed at her eyes. "Sixteen years ago, Orvie tried to tell me something, something about Mr. Maltravers and Mr. D'Amato, but I didn't listen. I was always sorry I hadn't. Right after that, Mr. D'Amato came up missing."

Peter and I exchanged quick glances.

"But this time, I listened," Mrs. Gleason continued. "It took a long time, but I finally figured out what he was trying to tell me."

"So she called Grandfather, and he called the police," Clare put in, letting go of Peter. "We all got here about the same time, but you were gone. We've been so worried."

The sheriff took a pad and ballpoint pen from his pocket. "If you'll just tell us what happened, Miss—"

"It was Mr. Maltravers," I told him excitedly. "He tried to kill us. Where is he? He mustn't get away."

"He won't be going anywhere," the deputy said. "He's dead. He wrecked his car down the road apiece on one of those slippery turns. I guess he was driving too fast through the storm."

"We've been trying to figure out what he was

doing here and why he left in such a hurry," said the sheriff. "Maybe you can tell us."

"How'd you know he was here? And what do you mean, he left in a hurry?" Peter asked.

"The front door was wide open," the sheriff replied. "He'd left his briefcase and his raincoat behind, too, and he'd knocked over the table in the hall. It looked like somebody was chasing him."

I closed my eyes and thought, *Well, Stephen, I guess Mr. Maltravers got to see you and Ellen, after all. And I bet you even played the piano for him, didn't you?*

"No," Peter said. "We wouldn't know anything about that."

The sheriff uncapped his pen. "Okay, so let's start from the beginning. You claim Mr. Maltravers tried to kill you. Just what did he do and why?"

"It's a long story," Peter said, with a sideways glance at me.

I knew what he was thinking, because I was thinking the same thing. We'd tell the story, but not quite *all* of it. The part about the ghosts of Ellen and Stephen would be a secret. Our secret— Clare's, Peter's, and mine.

Besides, Ellen and Stephen weren't here anymore. They were gone. I don't know how I knew. I just knew. They'd done what they'd set out to do, and Peter and I had helped them.

"Maybe we'd all better sit down, then," the sheriff suggested. "Mrs. Gleason, do you have any more of that good coffee?"

"Before we start, though," I said, "there's something I have to tell Clare. It's very important."

I went over to her and put my arms around her.

"Listen to me, Clare. Everybody's had it wrong all these years. Your parents loved you. They loved you very much. Your father didn't desert you, and your mother didn't commit suicide. They would never, never have done anything like that. Peter and I found out what really happened. It was Mr. Maltravers. Mr. Maltravers murdered your parents!"

Clare gasped, then burst into tears.

"Whaaaat?" shouted Mr. Hadley.

"Forget the coffee, Mrs. Gleason," barked the sheriff.

Just then the phone rang. It was Dad.

As I took the phone from Mrs. Gleason, I noticed for the first time that the electricity was back on. And now the phone was working. Was the old house trying to tell me something?

"I'll be there in less than an hour," Dad announced briskly. "I got an early start this morning and I've driven straight through. I'm at a gas station a few miles down the road. How do I get to Stoneycraig? Should I stop at Mr. Maltravers's office for directions?"

"No. No," I said hastily. "He's . . . not there. Just make a right turn at the little one-lane road after you pass the village green. It will bring you to Stoneycraig."

The excited babble at the kitchen table increased

in volume. Clare was clinging to Peter again and he was patting her shoulder. Like a brother. Or a cousin. Or a very, very good friend.

The look he gave me over her head, though, wasn't brotherly. I remembered that kiss back in the cave and my knees wobbled.

Oh dear, I thought. *But what about Clare? How will she feel when she realizes that she and Peter aren't . . .*

And then I thought, *But her life will be changed now. She won't feel so unloved and insecure anymore. As gorgeous as she is, she'll find at least a dozen guys to make her forget Peter. That girl has real killer-babe potential!*

Dad's voice brought me back to reality. "What's all that noise I hear in the background?" he asked suspiciously. "What are you kids up to?"

"Well, Dad—" I began.

"You're not throwing a wild party or anything, are you?"

"No, Dad, but—"

"I hope you haven't forgotten that I'm coming up there to write a book," he said. "That means you and your boisterous little friends are going to have to find another place to hang out."

"Yes, Dad, but—"

"Peace and quiet. That's what I was promised when I rented Stoneycraig. Peace and quiet," Dad went on. "I have a feeling you two have been staying up past midnight and listening to loud music and heaven only knows what else!"

"Yes," I said. "I guess that pretty much sums it

up. You're right. It *has* been pretty noisy around here."

I smiled across the room at Peter, my darling, my love, and he smiled back.

"But I give you my word, Dad," I said. "Stoneycraig's going to be a *very* quiet house from now on."

BEBE FAAS RICE, a 1994 Edgar Award–Nominee, has written over sixteen books for young readers. She lives in Falls Church, Virginia.

WHEN THE MOON IS IN THE SEVENTH HOUSE . . .

BEWARE

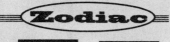

#1 STAGE FRIGHT (LEO)
Lydia loves the spotlight, but the stage she is on is set for danger.

#2 DESPERATELY YOURS (VIRGO)
Someone at Fairview High will do anything for attention, and they may give Virginia a *killer* deadline.

#3 INTO THE LIGHT (LIBRA)
The line is blurry between Lydia's reality and her fantasy-world mural. What happens when her mural is slated for destruction?

#4 DEATH GRIP (SCORPIO)
Sabrina wants to avenge her boyfriend's death, which she knows was no accident—but revenge can be costly.

CHECK OUT THESE HOT NEW SERIES

SAMANTHA CRANE...

**My So-Called Life *meets*
NYPD Blue *in this exciting new
series from the author of the
bestselling Freshman Dorm
books.***

**When you go to high school in
Hollywood, some kids have stars**

ROCK 'N' ROLL SUMMER

***When two guys join an all-
girl rock band, anything can
happen!***

**Frank and Eddie are having a
tough time launching their
musical careers... unitl they
hear about a gig in an all-girl
band. The**

REBEL ANGELS

***A group of teen angels strug-
gle
to earn their wings.***
**Serafina, Peter, Gabriel, Ezekiel,
and Anjelica died young and
went straight to heaven. But to
become full-fledged angels, the**

Four teens from different worlds star as ER volunteers in this new series.

Max, Dagger, Sara, and Kyle didn't know what they were made of—until they became volunteers in the ER. And it will take something extraordinary to force four

CODE BLUE

Vital signs are strong for four volunteers in the ER

C O D E

BLUE

IN THE EMERGENCY ROOM

LISA ROJANY

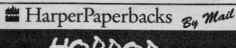